Libidissi

Libidissi

translated from the German
by John Brownjohn

Georg Klein

PICADOR

Originally published in German 1998 by Alexander Fest Verlag, Berlin

This translation first published 2001 by Picador
an imprint of Macmillan Publishers Ltd
25 Eccleston Place, London SW1W 9NF
Oxford and Basingstoke
Associated companies throughout the world
www.macmillan.com

ISBN 0 330 39241 7

1 3 5 7 9 8 6 4 2

A CIP catalogue record for this book is available
from the British Library.

Phototypeset by Intype London Ltd
Printed and bound in Great Britain by
Mackays of Chatham plc, Chatham, Kent

Libidissi

1 Derision

Here on the outskirts of the city, on the edge of its aerial springboard to my far-off homeland, I=Spaik am waiting for my successor. Prior notice of his arrival has propelled me out to the airport. I=Spaik have had myself conveyed by taxi from the rag-boilers' quarter of the Old City to the open-air steps of the airport terrace. I have yet to meet a foreigner who would risk driving to the periphery alone, nor do my long years of residence empower me to make for an outlying destination on my own and with any certainty of getting there. Immutably dismissive of outsiders, the city keeps me in a semi-touristic condition, employing this and still choicer ways of humiliating a foreigner who has long since lost his arrogance.

Not even native inhabitants are privileged to make their way through the inner districts with nonchalant ease. My handsome and, as luck would have it, one-eyed cabby had beads of sweat trembling above his puckered eyelid and his one remaining azure-blue orb when, after half an hour's drive, we suddenly resumed our walking-pace progress along one of those winding, skyless alleyways in which an overturned handcart is enough to bring the traffic to a standstill. It's no use yelling when you're stuck, still less

3

trying to press on or throwing the vehicle into reverse. You have to wait for the hapless tradesman to reload his wares with his own hands and the help of light-fingered locals. And patience, patience, self-derisive patience is what the destination-hungry foreigner requires when the carelessly reloaded merchandise, a tottering stack of video cassettes or a mound of hemp cakes, topples off for a second time, eludes its owner's grasp and eye, and goes slithering across the worn, mirror-smooth, precipitous roadway.

The roof garden of the airport restaurant is in a dilapidated state. The hand's-breadth cracks in the concrete floor are filled with wind-blown sand, the viewing platform lists towards the runways in the west. Sooner or later, not even the steel supports of later date will prevent the prestressed concrete structure from sagging. Yet the arrival and departure halls, a large-scale project designed and directed by a consortium of West European firms, were built during my own time here. The corrugated-iron hangars of the old airport erected by the occupying power continue to squat, incandescent in the setting sun, on the eastern edge of the new runways. Stretching away beyond them is the city: the hazy, shimmering ribbon of the corrugated-iron and canvas shanty town, the slate grey of the better-class suburbs, the dark agglomeration of the high-lying districts, and last of all, situated on three distant hills that merge into a single black hump, the Goto, the oldest part of the city and one we foreigners are forbidden to enter.

I=Spaik am drinking Zuleika-Cola, the foulest of the local beverages. All foreigners are served it as a local speciality. We expatriates, who always offer it to our rare visitors from home as a welcoming drink, relish the sight of them slurping it with a mixture of avidity and faint revulsion when told how *zuleika*, its alcoholic base, is made. Mare's milk fermented with the aid of bacteria supplied by the intestines of slaughtered calves is shaken until it curdles. This watery mush is then left to stand until it separates into curdlike paste and whitish liquid. The curds are used to fatten the small indigenous pigs; the milky, sweetish liquid, which is young *zuleika*, undergoes additional fermentation in cedarwood casks until, after a year, it attains the requisite alcoholic strength.

Pig-rearing and the brewing of *zuleika* were for centuries the exclusive preserve of the Egichaean minority. The Egichaeans, who cultivated remnants of a language of their own, were precluded from absorption into the larger ethnic groups by their curious religion. The religious faith that was eradicated from the city in company with the Egichaeans themselves should, I suppose, be termed Christian, although their belief in the coming of a second Messiah probably transcended what is generally termed the Christian faith. But the question has lost its relevance: no one here still believes in the advent of Egichaeus. During the disturbances that followed the occupying power's withdrawal, the Egichaeans were accused of having collaborated with the city's hated foreign masters more brazenly than anyone else, and the inhabitants of the Egichaean quarter were massacred at the very outset of the sanguinary struggle for power. A few of them managed to hide and escape aboard freighters anchored offshore. Such of these refugees as emigrated to the United States are reputed to have become fabulously wealthy in no time – at least, any local shopkeeper can tell you stories of Egichaean dollar millionaires. Impoverished families from the shanty town on the city's eastern outskirts took over the six-foot *zuleika* casks, the dwarf pigs in their backyard pens, and the murderously depopulated houses of the Egichaean quarter. Not in the least perturbed by the blood-spattered walls of their ethnically cleansed homes, the new arrivals contrived to carry on brewing *zuleika* and rearing the delicate little pigs with no appreciable loss of quality. Sarcastic foreigners are fond of pointing out that the new *zuleika* producers' activities are at odds with the traditional precepts of their orthodox forefathers, but this cheap jibe only shows how prone we are to misjudge the city and its happenings.

Today, or tomorrow at latest, my successor will be a perspiring reality. I learned only last night that he would be arriving within the next two days. My left eyelid, which has grown ever weaker during my years of foreign service, and now droops perceptibly, trembles whenever I=Spaik terrorize myself by picturing the man destined to succeed me: his solid flesh, loosely swathed in a lightweight cotton suit, his naively resolute tread on the treacherous roadways of the old quarters. This radiant individual fresh from home, this imbecile condemned to serve abroad, will be imprinted with preconceived notions, as I used to be, of what goes on here.

The last evening flight has landed. All the passengers have disappeared into the arrivals hall a few feet below my vantage point. There were only a dozen or so: a party of Japanese businessmen, a handful of American backpackers, and a lone fellow countryman. The city that has effaced so many of my memories of home has rendered me almost unbearably sensitive to my compatriots' physical characteristics. I=Spaik watched him through my binoculars as he walked unsteadily, head wobbling, down the gangway. One of the Japanese had to help him mount the running board of the electric bus. The German is corpulent, possibly suffering from heart trouble, but undoubtedly a man of around my own age, so he can't be my successor. The Bureau would never send a forty-year-old out here. I=Spaik am at liberty to rise and go. The only planes to land at night come from the south and east. There's no point in manning my observation post any longer.

The light is fading. My gaze travels once more over the deserted runways and comes to rest on the lights of the city. Bemused by the sudden remission of suspense, I=Spaik murmur its name, fumble blindly in my pillbox, wash down what I've extracted with a final swallow, and sense that the waiter is eyeing me contemptuously. Few locals would deign even to moisten their fingertips with *zuleika* in public. It's said to be customary for waiters in the cafés and bars of the nightclub district to spit in foreigners' glasses of Zuleika-Cola before serving them. My right hand drops some paper money beside the empty glass. Like any street trader, I keep both trouser pockets stuffed with hundred- and thousand-denomination notes crumpled into little balls. The inflation rate here beggars description. A parting glance at the cash I've left confirms that it will cover the bill and a tip. It includes at least one new five-hundred. The garish orange notes, a product of the latest currency reform, bear the likeness of the Great Gahis and are currently accepted even in the bars of luxury hotels and in Freddy's Steam Bath.

My cabby has been waiting for me. He sees me coming down the steps and shortcircuits his waiting colleagues by driving straight up to the entrance. The others start tooting, open their doors, and shout at him in the urban dialects and argots of which I=Spaik have only an imperfect grasp. I am, however, familiar with the principal terms of abuse and the derisive gestures that accompany them, although their full range of application will always exceed the limits of my knowledge. The driver of the foremost taxi, a preternaturally muscular man, has actually got out. He slaps the bonnet with the flat of his hand and incessantly bellows the same turn of phrase, a three-word synthesis that likens the target of his abuse to a degenerate, incestuous billy-goat of the local breed. Only when I=Spaik reach my taxi does its driver respond with a gesture which, though new to me, is instantly comprehensible. Inserting the little finger of his left hand in his mouth, he pumps it swiftly in and out, producing a sucking sound. His adversary promptly stops ranting, wipes his fair, spittle-flecked moustache on the back of his hand, turns away with a shrug, points to me with a pitying grin, and calls something to his fellow cabbies: a long, rolling word – a word of which I understand not a syllable, but one whose drift is now, to my instant embarrassment, beginning to dawn on me.

2 Poise

On the drive back, in the vast, deserted, transitional land-scape between the airport and the first properly built-up districts of the city, darkness falls. The refuse tips, the abandoned industrial installations, the tents and shacks of the poor, the whole environs of the motorway – everything disappears into the murk. Fires large and small, little camp fires and blazing mountains of garbage, are all that betray how the inhabitants of the periphery continue to exist. I= Spaik ask the cabby to take me to Freddy's Steam Bath in the former Egichaean quarter. Freddy's establishment is the only one foreigners can patronize with an easy mind. We, the city's permanent expatriates, form the nucleus of Freddy's clientele. The locals who go there do so primarily in order to show off a traditional steam bath to business associates from the West. When the latter pay their first and – usually – last visit to Freddy's place and finally venture into one of the slumbrous steam rooms, they often eye me curiously. They misconstrue the colour of my skin and the casual way in which my body reclines on its slab. Their investigative urge prompts them to mistake me, a long-time foreign resident, for native flesh, and I=Spaik have never sought to correct that misconception.

Before their conversion into a steam bath, so Freddy told me, the premises were used for the curing and cold storage of hams. A forgotten butcher's hook still dangles from the ceiling of one of the massage cubicles. The floors are older still. The mosaics in the lobby and the painted tiles surrounding the plunge pool indicate that the building was originally an Egichaean place of worship. The little coloured stones and the whole wealth of ornaments and symbols have been no more effaced by the wooden sandals in which Freddy's customers shuffle across the floors than they were by the pork butchers' clogs and the horny feet of the Egichaean worshippers of yore. These pictorial works have never tempted me to scrutinize them closely. Today, when I=Spaik bent down to knead the numb big toe of my right foot, I noticed for the first time that the changing room I've used for years is also adorned with a small mosaic: a lone figure picked out in little red and white stones and surrounded by a grey circle. A girl with one bare foot raised to reveal its sole, she's hurrying into the notional depths of the floor. Her elbows are widely splayed as if fending off the space around her by main force, and her head is turned at such an angle that one eye – three white stones and one red – is looking over her shoulder. While slipping my feet into their steam-room sandals, I=Spaik briefly wondered why the running girl's backward glance should still, after a lapse of centuries, prompt a chance observer to feel forsaken.

The decor of the baths, which is Freddy's work, bears witness to his unerring sense of style. He had the bulk of the fixtures and fittings removed from the erstwhile

officers' mess of the occupying power. The wooden columns adorned with paintings of female veil-dancers are
an object of particular and recurrent interest to the culture
vultures among his clientele. My naked back is resting
against the most colourful and substantial of these. Freddy
has made this splendid *unicum* the central column of his
aromatherapeutic steam room. Encircling it is an elegant
circular bench. I=Spaik have this to myself, the baths being
sparsely frequented so early in the evening. I look through
one of the little glass windows at the big, heart-shaped
plunge pool. A dozen of Freddy's houseboys are squatting
round it in their terry towels. Seen at this range through
clouds of steam and the irregularities of the old glass pane,
they are indistinguishable. All are boyishly slim, almost
undersized, and all have the same haircut, a short back and
sides that leaves their ears exposed. Each wears a gold
chain round his neck bearing a medallion engraved with
Freddy's 'F' and a three-digit number.

The lowest number I ever came across was 003, the
highest 243. I don't know what system Freddy uses when
numbering his houseboys, but there are never more than a
dozen of them, nor have I=Spaik ever known one to remain
in service for longer than three months. Many catch my eye
only once and have disappeared, never to be seen again, by
the time I come again. I remember the last 243 because he
spoke remarkably good French – peculiarly accented and
sprinkled with foreign words, to be sure, but fluent and
endowed with a wide vocabulary. He told me during a
massage that he came from the coast of West Africa. And,
while his hands pummelled my flesh, I became steadily

more accustomed to his African version of the ancient European tongue, with its wellnigh bellowed elisions, strangely displaced nasals, and abundance of supplementary gutturals. He and his two brothers had concealed themselves in an ill-ventilated container aboard an old cargo vessel. Extreme thirst had compelled them to drink their own urine for the last two days, but the long voyage had turned out well in the end, and he was glad to be working for Freddy. It would have been professionally advisable, or at least in keeping with the devotion to duty which my successor will doubtless wear on his sleeve, to question 243 more closely that night. The boy was talkative, and it is rare for any of the houseboys to be able to speak more than the few words of English or French they need for the job. But the young black was an exceptionally good masseur, and that steered my thoughts in another direction. The very next evening, the 243 medallion was dangling beneath another Adam's apple. Its new incumbent was one of the fair-skinned, freckled youngsters more and more commonly to be found among Freddy's houseboys in the last two years. I have heard these palefaces whispering together in Russian on several occasions, but they clam up at once when they notice I'm listening and play dumb as soon as I address them in my Russian, which is no less intelligible for being execrable.

Freddy enters the steam room. The sight of him never ceases to startle me. I=Spaik still wince at the disparity between his height and his emaciated frame. Here at the baths Freddy wears a towel round his waist, saronglike, and over it an open jacket of undyed silk. He has showered me with little courtesies throughout the years since my first visit to his establishment. As soon as I arrive a houseboy brings me, unasked, a chilled *zuleika* brandy and some local nibbles, among them the wickedly expensive three-year fruit of the fatnut tree. These half kernels can be readily mingled with my assortment of tablets, so chance determines which pills my fingertips pop into my mouth, one by one, in the course of a night at the baths. Freddy's attentions have gradually developed into more intimate marks of favour. For some time now, he has regularly brought me newly recruited houseboys of the type and age I prefer, youthful and muscular but not too skinny. Less than a year ago, on my fortieth birthday, he held a surprise party for me in the crypt beneath the steam rooms. Heaven alone knows how he discovered my date of birth, but the gathering included everyone whose half-naked presence I=Spaik can endure when in the same half-naked state. Freddy had not only assembled them all but, with his unfailing powers of discrimination, invited no one surplus to requirements.

Freddy has sat down on my left. Even when seated, and despite the curvature of his spine, he tops me by more than a head. Without more ado he starts to tell me about the Japanese who arrived on the evening plane. He has learned from his wondrously prolific sources that I=Spaik have just come from the airport, but he forbears to ask what prompted as immobile a person as myself to stray so far from the old quarters of the city. He discloses that one of the Japanese has been sent here on a special assignment. The party of businessmen in which I saw him is merely the base liquid with which he has been injected into the city. The

Japanese are here to demonstrate some new computer games, specially modified for the local market, to the whole-salers of the video souks.

My left ear itches. It senses that some useful information is being instilled into it. Freddy rests his right hand on my knee. I feel the pressure of his long, bony fingers through the towelling, and my dorsal muscles go taut. Freddy tells me the infiltrator's Japanese pseudonym and opines that the almond-eyed gentleman must have had to put in a lot of practice in order to pronounce it correctly. Then he divulges what the self-styled Japanese is called in his native United States. His two given names are so wonderfully American, so expressive of naive pride in the country's sanguinary genesis and its bloodstained heroes, that we can't refrain from testifying to their authenticity by giggling in unison.

Freddy rises to welcome some customers. My dorsal muscles relax. I shall spend the night here. The next plane my successor could take flies in from Istanbul late tomorrow morning. Freddy is shaking hands with the new arrivals. I=Spaik recognize my plump compatriot from the airport, who has walked over to the pool with the customer relations representatives of a local construction company. The bath towel wrapped around his body comes to within an inch of his nipples. Freddy is chatting to him, probably in Piddi-Piddi, the city's English-based lingua franca, an idiom that carries the source language's lack of inflection to extremes. In the case of nouns, for example, no distinction is drawn between singular and plural. The personal pronoun of the first person singular has disappeared com-pletely; instead, the speaker always refers to himself by whatever name his fellow conversationalist happens to call him. Piddi-Piddi is spoken with machine-gunlike rapidity and at maximum pitch. It is customary to bridge pauses for thought and achieve a wide variety of rhetorical effects by repeating words or phrases several times over, a stuttering form of delivery which I=Spaik began by practising with reluctance but now employ quite readily. Incorporated in the everyday vocabulary are a few hundred words borrowed from the local languages, mainly place names, swear words, and the names of dishes and drinks, all of which are uttered with an exaggerated, almost burlesqued American accent. All the local inhabitants strictly observe this unwritten rule, and the new arrival is strongly advised not to mimic the correct pronunciation of individual words. At the very least, any attempt to do so will be met with contempt and ostracism.

Freddy claims to be of mixed blood. His father, allegedly a local airline pilot, is said to have begotten him on a Maltese stewardess and given the boy a home when his mother died young. I=Spaik cannot tell how much of this actually happened. Freddy understands our trade. He's familiar with its colourful fictions, but also with the crass uniformity of its thought processes. It simply dawned on him at some stage, as it did on me, that any item of information, however abstruse, is preferable to no information at all. The myth of the paternal pilot entitles Freddy to let drop an occasional sentence in what is, statistically speaking, the country's principal language. This he does in the nasal drawl of the technocratic elite. I=Spaik once heard him speaking his putative mother's Maltese with a businessman from the island in question. But what counts for more with me than Freddy's gift of the gab is a slip he once made in my presence. It happened years ago, in the bright, glaring light of my early days here. An Armenian businessman was celebrating in the vault beneath the steam rooms the belated conclusion of an immensely complicated transaction. Big deals can be made in this city, but seldom in a quick and straightforward manner. The Armenian, a grizzled veteran of the international price war in semi-finished electronic products, was just describing the final tribulations of the deal, which had now been successfully clinched, when one of the houseboys, with a trayful of tumblers clutched to his chest, tripped and fell head first into their splintered remains. I=Spaik was standing close behind Freddy, so my ears were probably alone in hearing the muttered oath that escaped his lips. But, even if anyone else had heard it, none of the others present would have been capable of recognizing his words as German. Neither then nor later did Freddy intimate whether he knew I'd overheard him. But now and again, especially when he slips me some useful information, as he did tonight, I have a sneaking suspicion that he's making an old-fashioned, long-term investment in me, almost out of loyalty but ultimately because sometime, somehow, he plans to exploit our secret compatriotism.

3 Titillation

We made a detour, taking a route that Spaik could not have foreseen. The Bureau's operational directive had reached the two of us at training camp in Corsica. We were far from heartbroken at having to quit the course at once. On the contrary, you'd become more and more depressed by the daily drills, the soul-destroyingly innocuous repetitions. We both love the novelty of the unprecedented, the bright intensity of the real thing. A flying boat transported us to the coast of Cyprus overnight. From there we travelled by minibus to the capital's airport hotel, where a double room had been reserved for us.

We were met by a certain Herr Kuhl, no less a person than Spaik's long-time controller at the Bureau. He had flown to Cyprus to brief us in person, a unique proceeding. We had never heard of a controller in his position being sent abroad on official business. Indeed, it contravened one of the principles of exclusive supervision that we should come into such close contact with Spaik's personal controller. Taken aback, we exchanged a surreptitious smile and did our best to conceal how astonished we were. The briefing began right away. Kuhl had equipped our room with everything he needed. He showed us a video film of

Spaik's previous activities, which he projected on the bare wall above the double bed. The tape had been painstakingly, almost lovingly compiled from material spanning many years. Picture and sound were excellent, discounting a few exceptions. All that suffered from some minor shortcomings was the presentation. Kuhl talked too much. He seldom struck the right balance in his efforts to elucidate the film, often speaking over his own recorded voice and merely saying the same thing less well. What was more, we'd had to push the double bed aside. Whenever Kuhl knelt on it to indicate some piece of action with his telescopic pointer, he started to teeter on the yielding mattress and strayed into the beam of light from the projector.

We both noticed, of course, how old Spaik's controller was. Like many in-house operatives, he obviously used a rehydrating cream designed to maintain the moisture of the skin at a youthful level. He had also dyed his hair and had his dental enamel polished and resealed. From his gymnastics on the bed and his habit of interrupting himself, we estimated that Kuhl must be some five years past retirement age. We knew of nothing in regulations that warranted this, even for in-house personnel. The film and Kuhl's commentary led us to infer that Spaik had been controlled by him ever since his arrival in the city. Spaik's importance, his mysterious productivity and permanently precarious status must have annulled the normal, official course of events and preserved this ageing in-house operative from the inevitability of retirement.

We moved on as soon as the briefing ended. A freight plane was flying vaccination serum and medical equipment

to the city on behalf of a United Nations child relief agency.
From now on we were two Austrian ophthalmologists on a
three-day fact-finding mission for the World Health Organization. Kuhl had issued us with the usual basic set of
documents. The personal particulars that accompanied
them had been reduced to their bare essentials and could
easily be memorized on the flight. The small freight plane,
an elderly Russian turboprop machine, was elaborately
stacked with crates. Cut off from the two pilots, we sat at
the rear, where a double seat had been screwed to the bulk-
head beside a window. Immediately after take-off you got
out the Bureau's final directive, which Kuhl had handed us
in a sealed envelope. You inserted the diskette it contained
in our laptop, and we decoded the thrice-encrypted information. The final directive was brief and its meaning crystal
clear: no deviation from orders. We now understood what
Kuhl was not allowed to know – quite rightly – and
what, given that he must have suspected it, had made him
so timidly overzealous. We exchanged a nod and a smile:
old men's concerns were immaterial to us.

The diskette had a built-in thermochemical self-destruct
mechanism. It gave off a sweetish smell, almost like lilac, as
it glided out of the port in the laptop, and the surface had
gone warm and sticky. Touched by this traditional, nostal-
gically physical method of destroying information, we
started to dream of days gone by. It was over three years
since we had been taken on a guided tour of the Technical
Adaptations Section in the course of our training. There
they still sat, the cranky types who devised melting diskettes and similar technical aids. They had dwindled in

19

number, admittedly, but their laboratories and workshops continued to occupy the first of the Bureau's three underground levels. Our intake spent a day roaming this Aladdin's cave. The two of us began our tour by lingering with a cartographer, the last one in the section. He was very fat and very old, possibly over fifty, and had a big square room to himself. Every inch of wall space was plastered with historic town plans, much enlarged laser copies of drawings, engravings and prints. One or two large-scale specimens began just above the close-carpeted floor, ran the full height of the wall, and even trespassed on the ceiling.

We were spellbound as soon as we entered by a map affixed to the inside of the door. The old cartographer explained that this intricate pen-and-ink drawing represented the ground plan of a free imperial city of the Holy Roman Empire. On close examination, the serpentine entanglement of narrow streets made a surprisingly three-dimensional impression. The first thing that struck you was that a steep alleyway opened out into a funnel shape as it neared the top, and that the inner courtyards of the surrounding buildings swam into view and became visible in their entirety in a nonsensical but optically convincing manner. Every movement of the beholder's head caused the drawn surfaces, the half-timbered walls and cobbled roadways, to move and become displaced in a remarkable way. Thick, black, seemingly undifferentiated outlines and evenly hatched expanses of shadow distorted themselves into new partial views of surprising depth.

You discovered the façade of the town hall, of which all we had initially discerned was a kind of bird's-eye view of its roof and tower. The cartographer revealed that this plan embodied a twofold, historical representation of the town hall. In addition to the single-towered structure confronting us, it already depicted a twin-towered Renaissance building. This magnificent edifice still stood today, he said, whereas its medieval predecessor had been torn down and banished to the shadowy realm of vedutas and urban panoramas. We twisted and turned in front of the plan with singular eagerness, trying to find the right viewpoint, but it wasn't until you mounted an office chair and we carefully rotated the seat that you glimpsed, for one brief moment, the onion domes the artist had inserted as his vision of the future.

Gratified by our interest, the cartographer explained that he wanted to employ the principles of early modern perspectival displacement in a computer programme for the evaluation of satellite photographs. The requisite electronic equipment was stacked on a table in the centre of his room. On several screens he showed us aerial photographs of a treeless, almost desertlike plain. The computer programme on which he was working aimed to reveal the existence of industrial installations below ground. But the cartographer's enthusiastic expositions soon began to bore us. We might have understood him better now, with the benefit of experience, but Enforcement Branch personnel like us are seldom granted access to the workshops and laboratories, and the overweight cartographer has probably fallen prey to the latest efficiency drive and disappeared into the limbo of retirement.

The child relief aircraft, an antiquated machine even by

local standards, flew slowly at low altitude. The pilots did not disturb us once. Safely ensconced behind great stacks of medical freight, we sweated in the thermal overalls we'd been persuaded to wear because of misgivings about the freight compartment's heating facilities. When we unzipped them the air smelt of us, of the soap from the hotel, where we'd showered together, and of the fresh gel on our hair. Take-off had been considerably delayed, so we'd wandered around the airport and ended up in the hairdressing salon, where a Cypriot barber had trimmed our already close-cropped hair and shaved our necks.

We gained some idea of the city's vast extent when the turboprop banked and went into a long, lumbering turn. We saw the edge of its yellowish bell jar of smog, the meandering convolutions of the arterial roads, and the shimmering central districts, whose densely concentrated specks of light showed how replete with life they were even now, at this late hour. Peering out of the tiny window with our heads close together, we felt as keyed-up and excited as we used to be on our very first missions. Our crewcut temples touched, and the little bristles tickled as they interlocked like Velcro.

4 Enervation

I=Spaik have been compelled to go home in the middle of the night, driven from Freddy's Steam Bath by my fellow countryman. With the unerring nose of a foreigner fresh from the airport, he ran me to earth in the aromatherapeutic steam room and accosted me in raucous English. The fat man is an engineer specializing in ferroconcrete structures. I=Spaik would have been prepared to lend an ear to all that was on his mind, both professionally and personally, but my ear was not enough for him; he proceeded to pester me with questions about the city. Stubborn protestations of ignorance availed me nothing; he refused to leave me in peace. When I=Spaik resorted to giving him a thoroughly repulsive description of the bugs that lay in wait for foreigners' hyperglycaemic blood, even in the best hotels – indeed, in Freddy's Steam Bath itself – he seemed interested even in the most noisome details. My only recourse was to escape into the nocturnal streets.

This is the third time I=Spaik have endeavoured to find my way home without a local's assistance. It must be possible to cover the route on foot. It should only take me a good hour, or an hour and a half at most, but first I have to cross the edge of the former Egichaean quarter, and that constitutes a special kind of barrier. Here, the houses were erected in two continuous rows, back to back, one facing the quarter inhabited by the Egichaean minority, the other the surrounding city. Four or five storeys high, the crude mud-brick buildings form a solid belt more than fifty feet wide. No streets traverse this cordon. The only routes in or out of the quarter are tunnel-like passages that run through the interiors of two buildings, an old Egichaean house and its counterpart on the other side.

On the way to Freddy's place my cabby had entered the walled part of the city via the tinsmiths' souk, a popular route familiar to me from numerous taxi rides. The sky in the tinsmiths' quarter is completely invisible, the entire thoroughfare being roofed over with beams and plastic sheeting. The wares suspended from this makeshift canopy almost brush the tops of passing cars. Continually brought to a halt, the two opposed streams of traffic crawl past the craftsmen's workshops and stalls. The tinsmiths work almost exclusively with waste metal. Much of their material derives from the vast numbers of imported cars consumed by the city. Nowhere in the world do motor vehicles wear out as quickly as in the murderous local traffic. Not even the most robust engines attain anywhere near their normal life expectancy. Many people assign responsibility for this to the fine, unfilterable, wind-blown sand and the painfully slow progress of traffic in the old quarters' narrow streets, some of which are incredibly steep; others blame the rapid wear and tear on the recklessly inconsiderate driving habits to which the locals cling in defiance of all common sense.

Last night, as I=Spaik crawled through the tinsmiths'

souk in the back of my taxi, street traders who recognized me as a foreigner and potential customer beat a tattoo on the windows with traditional products of local craftsmanship: ornate *zuleika* carafes, potbellied hubble-bubbles, and, arrayed on long strings, little rods with a copper or gold ball at either end, sexual aids that can be inserted in a perforation beneath the glans to enlarge the diameter of the erect penis.

All such objects are familiar to me to the point of tedium. None of those wares, not even an apparent novelty made of sheet aluminium and copper wire, would have tempted me under normal circumstances. But my time at the airport, the trepidation with which I had awaited my successor's arrival and my relief at his temporary failure to turn up – the whole torment of suspense, in fact – had worn me down. My powers of resistance were eroded by the street traders' rhythmical drumming on the taxi's roof and their swift alternation of imploring and imperious grimaces. My eye, which had once more been spared the sight of my successor, weakened. A bizarre object, slowly and artfully dangled in front of the windscreen by a hand from above, seemed in some vague but compelling way to aspire to become my property. The owner of the hand was obviously lying, belly down, on the roof of the taxi. To buy something from this exceptionally importunate salesman would undoubtedly disperse some of the surrounding crush, so I= Spaik lowered the window, knocked on the roof, and was handed the object in question. My left hand reached for it, my right hand paid for it, and the new acquisition was lying in my lap. It was an intricate pendant, a species of necklace. Despite myself, I=Spaik was so ambivalently pleased by its scintillating colours that I spread my fingers and held it up before my eyes once more. It had been fashioned with fine pincers and a soldering iron, undoubtedly under a magnifying glass, from the innards of electronic equipment. Its delicate filigree of wires, resistors, and miniature diodes and transistors formed a glittering kaleidoscope of polished precious metals and multifarious enamels. The letters and numerals garishly imprinted on the diminutive cylinders and rectangles seemed to suggest that, even in their new environment, the structure of a piece of jewellery, the components had to fulfil some technological function.

Like my two previous ventures, tonight's attempt to reach home on foot is ending in disaster. Helplessly, I survey the dark house fronts. I'm positive that the route from the Egichaean quarter into the tinsmiths' souk has to be somewhere in this few hundred yards of street. The characteristic din, the discordant clatter and gonglike notes of beaten metal and the blare of radios, comes drifting across a somewhat lower pair of back-to-back houses, but there's no way through. At the same time, my powers of recall torment me with a detailed mental picture: the building that gives access on the Egichaean side is very old, windowless, and constructed of blue clay. On entering it one is plunged in shimmering gloom. The tunnel's bulging, sagging roof seems close enough to touch. There is only one traffic lane, and halfway along it the narrow roadway is still further constricted by one wing of a double gate. The taxi's sides almost brush the soot-stained timbers, and the cold, olfactory residue of the arson that scorched them seems to infiltrate the vehicle's interior. But then comes the lighter, wider half, and an instant later one emerges into the tinsmiths' souk, where innumerable gas lamps with chromium-plated reflectors generate a harsh white glare.

Total darkness has never flowed to meet me even in the Old City's remotest byways. This may be because of the particle-laden dome of smog that overhangs the central districts and reflects enough of a glow to illuminate unlit corners. I=Spaik make another attempt to tell the mud-brick houses apart by their nocturnal colour. Blue clay buildings like the one I seek are rare, even in the Egichaean quarter. They're supposed to be among the oldest multi-storey residential buildings in the world. I found it almost objectionable at first that the blue clay's mixture of pigments should have preserved its luminosity for centuries, surpassing comparable materials or coats of paint in clarity of colouring. This certainly applies in sunlight, but also in the harsh glare of the mercury vapour lamps with which many streets, the one in which I live included, are illuminated after nightfall. The blue clay becomes totally unrecognizable only in the treacherous lighting of the Egichaean quarter, where small petroleum lamps flickering on a level with the third-floor windows cast a rancid orange-yellow light that bathes every frontage in shades of brown of varying degrees of ugliness.

I'm rescued by a taxi. A huge American limousine of long-obsolete design comes towards me, the front wings overarching its big wheels like bloated cheeks. A massive radiator grille yawns between the bonnet and the bumper.

Its serrated, chrome-plated teeth, reminiscent of the peculiar dentition of various predators, combine to create an air of potent menace. Now, seated in the right-hand corner of the rear seat, in a dip in the much repaired leatherette upholstery, I can hear almost nothing of the big-capacity engine that must lurk behind those gleaming teeth. Probably of recent manufacture, it may well be the fifth or sixth power plant to do duty beneath the bonnet. Although the inhabitants of this city wear out gadgets at a dizzy rate, they preserve the historic outer shells of some machines with elaborate care.

My driver soon reaches the exit from the Egichaean quarter, which turns out to be only a few doors beyond the place where I=Spaik gave up looking. We quickly traverse the tinsmiths' souk, which is now, after midnight, a little less busy than it was. Crossing Freedom of Speech Boulevard, where the bombastic buildings of the country's erstwhile rulers have since been overtopped by one or two glass-encased skyscrapers, we enter the district in which I= Spaik have lived for so long. A foreigner can live quite well in the former rag-boilers' quarter, and several hundred of us have taken lodgings in this old and rather unprepossessing part of the city. Many, especially the Americans, favour the side streets leading off the boulevard. My own residence is situated in the real heart of the quarter, where the rag-boilers' little two-storeyed houses enclose square courtyards that still contain the troughs once used for making paper in the traditional manner. My back room overlooks a courtyard of this kind. Growing in its three low troughs is a dense clump of thorny, thistle-like plants. In winter, when a lot of rain has fallen, this thicket takes only a few days to explode into white blossom. Then every stem bears dozens of small, cinnamon-scented florets that promptly attract a multitude of flying, crawling insects. For weeks thereafter the soft and rubbery capsules litter the courtyard like a slowly greying carpet, until, without germinating, they become assimilated into the grime that coats the yard's mud floor.

Reluctantly, my body heaves itself out of the ancient limousine. I=Spaik haven't worn a watch for years, but my sensitivity to the city's pulse tells me that it can't be much past midnight. It goes against the grain to return home so early. I only occupy the first floor of the little house, leaving the ground floor empty. Obedient to a habit of many years' standing, I linger at the foot of the stairs and doze in an absurdly obstinate way. I don't know what inhibits me, again and again, from climbing them immediately. It may be the smell of the wooden staircase that stupefies me. Many's the time when I=Spaik awake with an aching back to find myself stretched out on one of the lower treads. Sleep seems to be overcoming me again in spite of my early night: my eyes close, my muddled thoughts encounter no resistance. But then I'm jolted out of my doze by a rattling sound that steadily swells in volume and terminates in a metallic thud. My torpor is dispelled at once. It's rare these days, distressingly rare, for me to receive a communication by pneumatic post. When this does happen, as it has tonight, I feel utterly exhilarated. My feet stumble up the last few stairs. I=Spaik hurry through the two darkened rooms to the reception hatch on the windowless south-facing wall. My tremulous fingers withdraw the brass bolt that secures the aluminium flap. The last of the pressure escapes with a hiss, and the pneumatic post projectile, a fat metal cylinder some nine inches long, its lightly oiled surface warmed by the friction of its journey, slides out into my waiting hands.

5 Nostalgia

I=Spaik stack all the pneumatic post capsules I receive on a shelf behind my television set. Its black case sets off the silvery array to good effect, and the close juxtaposition of the identical cylinders makes my collection look bigger than it is. Every capsule consists of two halves, each of them open at one end. The shorter half, which acts as a closure, can be screwed to its counterpart by means of a spiral thread three finger-widths in extent. The polished metal of both halves is smooth and unadorned except on the ends, which bear the deeply impressed trademark of a firm based in my own country: three intersecting rings arranged in a triangle. Anyone who cares to inspect this logo can find it all over the city. The cast-iron manhole covers in Freedom of Speech Boulevard display it, as does each of the massive hexagonal-headed bolts that secure the rails of the Old Municipal Railway to their sleepers. The street urchins know of the trademark's exotic provenance. Grabbing foreigners by their trouser legs or camcorder straps, they tow them over to the oval hydrant covers on which the entwined rings, only slightly worn away by the urban traffic, can be seen with exceptional clarity.

Tonight's pneumatic post capsule refuses to open. This

happens once every two or three transmissions, but the two halves soon free themselves if one trickles some sesame-seed oil into the join and carefully taps the threaded section on the edge of a table. Only once, right at the start of my pneumatic post correspondence, did I=Spaik lose my temper and slit open a capsule lengthwise. It's a mystery why my house, a modest brick building that used to be the home and workplace of a family of rag-boilers, should have been connected to the system. The reception hatch did not come to light until some weeks after I moved in, when a pest controller, a member of the Cyrenian ethnic group, took down an old tapestry in search of lurking cockroaches. I=Spaik, being an ignorant foreigner, had no idea what type of installation it was. Having, in turn, tapped the emblem on the flap and my chest with the nozzle of his poison spray, the cockroach hunter explained in Piddi-Piddi that this was one of the few pneumatic post terminals still intact. Since I hailed from the home of this technology, he declared, I had a responsibility to make use of it.

With the touching enthusiasm of a novice, I devoted the ensuing weeks to gathering information about the system. In the archives of *The Voice of Liberation*, the city's only newspaper, which house its past editions and those of its predecessor, I found a few details of the network's construction and early utilization. I recognized the erstwhile pneumatic post office, a colonnaded block in one of the irremediably turgid, transitional *fin de siècle* styles, from a photograph. This building had already caught my eye at the south end of Freedom of Speech Boulevard, if only because of its singularly hideous appearance. On the off chance, I=Spaik went to investigate. The former pneumatic post office now housed an institute devoted to the study and preservation of the oral traditions of desert and steppe tribes close to extinction. There I was greeted by a public relations officer who informed me, briefly but politely, that the pneumatic post company had gone bankrupt soon after its foundation. The main technical installations, foremost among them the elaborate system of compressed air terminals, had been randomly dismantled and scrapped in the ensuing decades, probably without exception.

Freddy, whom I=Spaik questioned on the subject some nights later, told me that this was essentially correct. It should, however, be noted that the official closure of the system had immediately preceded the first national purification campaign launched by Gahis, then a very young man. This was when his white-robed adherents had first appeared outside pavement cafés and, in broad daylight, emptied foreigners' glasses of *zuleika* on the ground at their feet. From the very first, Freddy went on, the Gahists made it their practice to tear off the flabbergasted foreigners' trousers and compel them to use those garments to mop the *zuleika*-spattered flagstones. Any locals caught drinking *zuleika* fared far worse. He, Freddy, had been forced to look on while a businessman of his acquaintance, a respected horsemeat dealer, had the hand that had held his glass sliced off with a traditional reed-cutter's knife in the gutter outside the Hotel Esperanza.

This drastic initial phase went on for a good three years, and before long no innkeeper or tradesman dared to offer *zuleika* for sale in public. This was also the period when the legendary Agoman family's black-market dealings in *zuleika* enabled it to amass its proverbial wealth. Under the management of one of old Ammon Agoman's sons, who had studied engineering in Berlin, the wrecked pneumatic post terminals were rendered serviceable again. Indeed, new channels of communication were opened up. Agoman Junior was ingenious enough to make exclusive use of tubular systems already embedded in the compressed air ducts. In particular, the hard-wearing and extravagantly capacious ceramic pipes of the very first sewage system, which dated from the last century, were employed to carry the now clandestine mail. The size of *zuleika* bottles was standardized so that they would fit perfectly inside a pneumatic post capsule. Another practice that hailed from the prohibition era was to bottle *zuleika* in unsightly but unbreakable PVC.

The ban on *zuleika* was disregarded almost overnight when Gahis's disciples committed mass suicide in the football stadium. Smuggling and the illegal trade in *zuleika* collapsed. The Agomans fought sanguinary battles for a share of their accumulated wealth. For a short while, cousins and cousins of cousins actually sent each other time-bombs by pneumatic post. Before long, however, one of old Ammon Agoman's grandsons skilfully succeeded in reconciling the rival branches of the family, almost all of whose members emigrated by degrees to the United States or Canada. No one could say exactly what had happened to the ownerless pneumatic post system after that. Terminals in various parts of the city were taken over by local gangs, but it was probable that they had no real idea what to do with them.

Such was Freddy's version, recounted in the vaporous atmosphere of the aromatherapeutic steam room, and I had nothing in the way of first-hand knowledge to add to it until, one night, a dream that confronted me with a distressingly complete set of visual memories of the old days at home was interrupted by the rattling approach and metallic thud of a pneumatic post capsule. Jolted out of my nightmare, I=Spaik found myself lying, as I sometimes do to this day, curled up at the foot of the stairs in the unused ground floor of my little house. I knew at once what had woken me. It had happened at last! I=Spaik scrambled to my feet and hurried upstairs. My first consignment – I unscrewed the two halves of the capsule with trembling hands – was a bottle of *zuleika*, nothing more. But, when I sampled a swig straight from the plastic bottle, I experienced an incomparably bitter taste surpassing absinthe in ambiguity, and my nostrils were assailed by the quasi-putrescent bouquet of vintage *zuleika* brandy, which instantly summons up thoughts of higher things. Distilling *zuleika* is difficult enough, but the imponderable nature of its micro-organic components entails that only small quantities of the spirit can be successfully stored and matured for years. Anyone wishing to acquire some not only needs connections among the families who produce it but has, in any case, to pay an outrageously high price in hard foreign currency. I finished off my first bottle of *zuleika* brandy, the entire contents of the half-litre bottle sent me by pneumatic post, the very same night. It wasn't until noon the next day, on awaking from a drunken sleep, that I=Spaik discovered the message accompanying the gift: the label was loosely stuck on at an angle and could easily be detached from the plastic bottle. Some information had been written in pencil on the back: the first communication addressed to me and sent by pneumatic post.

I get the capsule open at last. A dent in the thread has prevented me from unscrewing it and tried my patience for an exceptional length of time. Like the last two communications, this one is inscribed on a strip of black rubber. The curl in the material suggests that the sender has cut the inner tube of a bicycle tyre into rectangles of appropriate size. One side of the black rubber is covered with white lettering. All the written communications that have reached me from the bowels of the pneumatic postal system display the same feature: an almost unjoined-up, schoolboyish handwriting of the sort I myself learned decades ago, while chewing my fountain pen. My correspondent has preserved the clarity and regularity of his youthful handwriting. His long-time adherence to it is betrayed by only minor deviations from this calligraphic norm.

The very first message I found on the back of the bottle label was as laconic as all its successors. The length and style of tonight's communication are no exception. All such notes dispense with a conventional preamble and conclusion, and the text, which numbers three sentences at most, is invariably suggestive of an official memorandum. Only one development has struck me over the years: spelling mistakes are on the increase. Many seem curiously archaic, as if hinting with subtle humour at some historical set of circumstances, but most lack any obvious significance and merely cause me to fear that a slow degenerative process is impairing the assurance with which the writer applies the rules of orthography.

I=Spaik am aware how much my humble self owes to the suggestions of my great pneumatic post correspondent. His very first message, which merely announced the establishment of a regular mail service, was a hint which my brain, trained in an altogether different way, instinctively comprehended. Every subsequent communication has been of importance to my continued presence in the city, and it was only at first that I sometimes felt slightly ashamed and embarrassed when it dawned on me how I=Spaik pored over the meagre sentences like the devotee of some oracle. The last and penultimate messages referred to my successor's impending arrival, but tonight's is the first to lend fitting orthographic expression, by means of a spectacular spelling mistake, to my imminent removal from office. For the first time ever, my long-established informant has distorted a word to the point of unrecognizability: only half the letters in his misspelling of the word 'liquidation' are correct.

In the early years of my pneumatic post correspondence, I=Spaik tried several times to get in touch with those who operated the system in the rag-boilers' quarter. My honest and correspondingly maladroit attempts to locate them were exploited by unscrupulous individuals who cheated me out of small sums of money. For some time, a young man turned up weekly to collect a charge for the connection, until one morning I found him beaten senseless outside my front door. His left ear had been sliced off, wrapped in cling film, and stuffed into the breast pocket of his shirt. On three occasions, conmen of similar calibre conducted me to places they claimed to be the pneumatic post office of the rag-boilers' quarter. Twice I=Spaik found myself abandoned in backyards enclosed by ruined buildings that betrayed no hint of their alleged function, and once I was guided by an adolescent boy to an *ognum*, a former prayer-house of the Gahist sect. The interior of the unpretentious rotunda was daubed from floor to ceiling with the familiar red purification symbols, but the floor itself was buried beneath an ankle-deep layer of putrescent goat dung.

6 Contemplation

We landed at first light on the city's former military airfield, where our papers were examined by officers of the People's Militia. Your failure to suppress a smile at the Moustaches' grim attention to detail rendered them twice as thorough when they spotted it. The suspicious militiamen made us remove our shoes – they even explored the seams of our outer clothing – and ended by photocopying every page of our Austrian passports, covers included. They refused for no stated reason to order us a taxi from the city, so we had to wait for the turboprop's freight to be loaded aboard a truck belonging to the child relief agency. There was just room for us and our bags on the tailboard, and so, as the sky paled, we drove into town over every conceivable kind of road surface and absence thereof.

We knew from Kuhl's briefing that the city boasted of being the oldest continuously inhabited settlement in the area. Although its claim to that superlative was contested by two other places, it was, beyond dispute, the oldest metropolis in this part of the world. Its slave market, long ago commended by classical authors for the abundance, variety and quality of its wares, had been captured on silver iodide plates by the earliest globe-trotting photographers.

Kuhl's informative video included some fine details from these historic daguerreotypes.

In the back of the truck, with the road unreeling beneath our eyes like an arrow-straight ribbon, we started to converse in Piddi-Piddi. Despite the skill of the language teacher assigned to us at the training camp in Corsica, our efforts to master the local vernacular had been inspired by devotion to duty alone. Now that we were in its place of origin, however, we suddenly found it easy to adhere to Piddi-Piddi's strict rules of simplification and intersperse its bastardized English with a few indigenous words. The driver of the truck sped over the atrocious road surface with no consideration for his load. Notwithstanding its six lanes, the motorway between the airport and the outskirts of the city was unworthy of the name. The windows of the wrecked cars that flanked it glittered in the light of the rising sun. Here and there, gutted tanks and other military hardware could also be seen. We drew each other's attention to the choicest specimens and practised our Piddi-Piddi by describing them. All at once it seemed to us a frivolous, childishly frolicsome language, the very nature of whose stuttering delivery infuses it with gusto and élan.

The desk clerk at the Hotel Esperanza, where the child relief agency was supposed to have booked us a double room, professed to know nothing of any such reservation. We went to work on the man in our arrival-happy Piddi-Piddi; he, for his part, stubbornly dismissed our claims in almost perfect French. But we were fresher than the desk clerk, who betrayed unmistakable signs of night-shift fatigue. His French steadily deteriorated and became defective as the argument wore on, and he eventually expressed a willingness to make two small attic rooms available to us. When we continued to rattle away, repeatedly insisting on our reservation and bombarding his overtaxed ears with as many indigenous words as possible, he suddenly recalled that the hotel's telephone lines had been temporarily out of order. Having rummaged in a wire basket full of crumpled faxes, he came upon one whose text he studiously hid from view. It was garbled, he said, but he had now contrived to decipher it: the South Oriel Suite had, after all, been reserved for us.

The rooms looked almost exactly as they had in the video film Kuhl showed us in Cyprus. Spaik's controller had eked out the short movie sequence with numerous stills. These photographs, which were underexposed and badly blurred by camera shake, had been electronically enhanced and their details blown up at the Bureau, but the colours were so distorted and the outlines of objects rendered so indistinct by underexposure that only Kuhl's commentary had enabled us to recognize, say, a bedside light or a bidet bowl.

The video had been shot years ago, and without an eye to intelligence-gathering, by a Belgian businessman. Spaik had moved into the South Oriel Suite on arrival and was supposed to make long-term use of the hotel's special facilities. The Belgian had met him in the hotel bar and accompanied him upstairs to drink the rest of the night away. In one shot, three bottles and two glasses could be seen standing close together on a coffee table with a very shiny surface. This blurred still life was followed by the sequence depicting Spaik himself. First, he intruded from above into the camera's rectangular excision from the table, though all that could be seen of him was one bare arm and part of his chest in a yellowish, presumably white, string vest. Then the camera panned upward to show Spaik seated on the sofa. The Belgian handicam operator, who was probably very drunk by now, had managed to keep almost the whole of Spaik's body in shot for three seconds or so. Visible were the bare knee and dark, hirsute thigh, the torso deeply embedded in the sofa's upholstery in under-pants and string vest. Both garments looked unattractively tight, as if bought for someone with a trimmer figure – as if Spaik had become bloatedly corpulent during his brief sojourn in the city.

The Bureau acquired this videotape only a few weeks ago, in the course of an international exchange of in-formation. It was the only document that afforded the authorities at home a visual insight into Spaik's life in the city. In a hesitant voice, Kuhl had commented on the adverse way in which Spaik's face had changed within a few weeks. Indeed, he went so far as to pronounce him almost unrecognizable. In our objective view, there could be no question of this. The Spaik of the video undoubtedly looked older and curiously puffy in the face, but it is common knowledge that most Europeans and North Americans find it difficult at first to adjust to the city's climate. We therefore proceeded on the assumption that the Spaik we sought, having become inured to local conditions, would look more like his earlier photographs.

We spent our first hour in the hotel strolling barefoot, this way and that, across the thickly carpeted floor of our suite.

So far as we could see, little had changed since Spaik's time at the Esperanza: the television had been replaced with a more modern set and the international assortment of miniatures in the minibar was twice as extensive. You quickly detected two antiquated microphones, one of Czech and the other of Israeli manufacture, both amateurishly installed and encrusted with greasy dust and dead flies. The monitoring device discovered by Spaik in the bedroom had been ripped out, and no one had even troubled to conceal its former location. A favourite hotel with Europeans and Americans since the day it opened, the Esperanza smelt almost obtrusively of our kind, of the intense exertion customarily exuded by our breed. You evinced a certain understanding of the fact that Spaik had gone in search of somewhere else to live, but there is no denying that his departure for a private address kept secret from the Bureau was the first of his serious derelictions of duty.

After lingering for some time under the shower, which we adjusted so that it ran wonderfully hot at first, and then, to invigorate ourselves, almost ice cold, our damp bodies crawled into bed. The whole of the bedroom, including the ceiling, was hung with a dark red, rose-patterned wallpaper. We had drawn the curtains, and the palm-sized blossoms and their thorny, winding stems looked deceptively three-dimensional in the gloom. Reaching for the roses above our heads, we found that the paper was unusually heavily embossed. The vegetation's stiff stems were raised like a bas-relief, and the illusion of corporeality was heightened by a half-matt, half-glossy finish. We suddenly found it an effort to confine our pillow talk to

Piddi-Piddi. The sight of the wallpaper encouraged us to lapse into our native tongue. It was as if the roses had imprinted the paper with some cosy reminder of old Europe – a whiff of their scent, perhaps. And so, after chatting awhile with our eyes closed, we fell silent and listened to the pleasantly unintelligible, fluctuating murmur that came to our ears through the walls and windows of the suite.

Outside, the noonday heat was approaching its zenith, intensified by a dry, scorching easterly wind which even euphemistic guidebooks call murderous, but which the multilingual literatures of the region have always extolled as stimulating. If they are to be believed, this anabatic wind can inspire the local inhabitants to make love with the utmost ardour. The two of us preferred to doze, or possibly sleep, before devoting the afternoon, the evening, and, if need be, the night, to looking for Spaik.

7 Determination

I=Spaik had been warned. Until dawn, fear impelled me to get out all the pneumatic post communications I had received over the years and study them repeatedly. Just as I had at the very outset, at the time of the earliest transmissions, I=Spaik searched for clues to the identity of the sender, who had remained anonymous to this day. What really underlay all this cogitation on my part was a single desire: to rob the warning I had received of its urgency by some feat of logical deduction that would divest my well-wisher of his magical anonymity.

Now, in the noonday heat, I've finally abandoned my futile efforts. With trembling hands, I toss my shaving things into a grimy plastic sponge bag. It has hung untouched for years, ever since I moved in, on a hook beside the bathroom mirror. Filthy, dust-coated hairs straggle across its quilted surface. I had completely forgotten the sponge bag's existence and its singularly hideous floral design. It never occurred to me in my routine daydreams, in the even tenor of my life in this alien city, that I would ever use it again to carry shaving things and soap.

Lieschen is climbing down the ladder into the living room. The rungs creak softly under her cautious tread.

Lieschen wears orthopaedic boots with hobnailed soles. She has never – not, at least, in my presence – stumbled or fallen over, even though she learnt to walk upright very late on. Lieschen lives in my attic. It's customary in this city to keep chickens on the roof. Small, almost bald, and repulsively ugly to Western eyes, the local hens are great destroyers of pests, and an ancient superstition insists, in defiance of religions of all kinds, that they promote the prosperity of the household to which they belong. The top floor of most houses, including those of recent date, is consequently surmounted by a waist-high roof space or attic to which the birds can retire at night and in the heat of the midday sun. This attic above my living quarters was unoccupied when I first moved in. Just occasionally, when it was invaded by one of the rats that come up from the river after dark, some of the chicken droppings that had rotted away to a powder would drift down through the cracks between the joists and land on my bed, my television set, or my wickerwork television armchair.

When Lieschen came to live with me, she suggested moving in up there. I=Spaik made a ladder with my own hands, forced open the dung-encrusted hatch in the ceiling, and helped her to clean out the roof space. The uppermost layers of chicken dirt could be swept up or scraped off with little difficulty, but we had to use screwdrivers to dislodge the rock-hard deposits of earlier times. It took us days of hard labour to expose every inch of the dark, cedarwood floorboards. Lieschen bought her household necessities from the shopkeepers of the neighbourhood: a thick hemp mat to sleep on and a two-ring oil stove on which to cook regional dishes of millet and rice. Her small television set is hooked up to my satellite receiver. Although she must have acquired one or two more household goods since moving into the roof space, I=Spaik have never again squeezed through the narrow hatchway since our grand spring-clean, so I cannot tell what further improvements Lieschen has made to her cramped little domain.

Having descended the ladder, Lieschen promptly sits down in my television chair. Her thin body, which is probably underweight for her age, makes mock of such a large piece of furniture. Only her orthopaedic boots are in surprising harmony with its clumsy design. My television chair was a birthday present from Freddy. Woven in traditional fashion from osiers and reeds, the thronelike seat was originally made to measure for the imposing rump of an officer in the forces of occupation. Inserted in the wickerwork are ornaments of carved horn, seashells, and painted slivers of bone, and the seat itself is upholstered in soft, slightly teased goatskin. When Lieschen and I watch television together, there's plenty of room for her to sit beside me in this baronial armchair – in fact she can even tuck up her clumsy boots on the cushion without our touching.

Lieschen has come down from her attic to watch *German Fun* with me. The programme goes out daily on the International Joy Channel between 11.00 and 11.25 a.m. It's supposed to be the first of my duties to watch *German Fun* every day, but since every message from the Bureau is repeated twice, or on three successive days, it's good enough if the polka arrangement of our national anthem

rings out in my home only every other morning. Sometimes, like yesterday and the day before, I=Spaik miss two
broadcasts on the trot, not only overnighting at Freddy's
Steam Bath but spending the morning there as well, or
taking a taxi from there to the Naked Truth Club in Freedom of Speech Boulevard.

Lieschen's TV-watching habits permit me this degree of
laxity where my official duty to remain in touch is concerned. She never misses a single broadcast of *German Fun*,
and has taken a great shine to Heinz, the presenter. Her
eyes devour all his facial contortions with the utmost
gravity. Heinz is a third-generation Australian of German
stock. His ancestral German is almost incomprehensible to
viewers in the old country, but long-time expatriates
delight in his strangled vowels. I=Spaik have more than
once seen fellow countrymen of mine, hard-boiled dealers
in every kind of merchandise, weep with laughter when
Heinz cracks one of his pathetic jokes. Heinz compères a
twenty-five-minute pot-pourri of sketches, commercials,
and pop music clips. He wears black cords with braces and
red leather flies, and whenever he touches his gold fly
buttons with the second and third fingers of his left hand a
message from the Bureau appears in the next commercial.
Lieschen, who knows this too, informs me whenever Heinz
fingers his flies. Actually, she could record the commercial
and the official message it contains, but I=Spaik am still
loath to entrust her with that task. The girl and I have
preserved a salutary distance despite our long cohabitation,
and it's inadvisable to share every last official secret with an
outsider.

Messages are recorded and deciphered by the same piece of equipment, a decoder plugged into the output socket on the front of my television set. Superficially it resembles an antiquated Walkman, but the battered plastic case conceals an assembly of relatively up-to-date modules. The Bureau's boffins were still granted a great deal of latitude in the days when my kind of agent went off to work in the cities of the Near East. This was the Indian summer of the fiddler and tinkerer. Kuhl explained the niceties of the gadget to me with almost rapturous precision, and I, too, derive a certain pleasure from using the decoder to this day. I have never managed to detect the relevant place on the soundtrack of a *German Fun* commercial. The decoder records it all and deciphers the section that carries the message while recording is in progress. The original soundtrack breaks off with a lip-smacking noise, and an electronically attenuated voice tells me what the Bureau wishes to impart. It is Kuhl's voice, digitally processed. Although it sounds comically high-pitched and has a technologically nasal quality, vestiges of Kuhl's natural intonation betray his characteristic mode of speech.

Lieschen extracts the remote control from under the cushion and switches on. We're only just in time. The last few lurching bars of the mazurkaized national anthem end with a hissing flourish of cymbals, then Heinz appears. As usual, the programme opens with an angled shot of him from below. His televised body begins at the lower extremity of his crotch and ends in the middle of his forehead. Heinz's feet have never yet come into shot, and his knees, too, are seldom to be seen – never, in fact, except when he underscores a particularly gross wisecrack by slapping his thighs with his huge hands. Only in the course of the programme does the camera pan up to reveal the buttercup yellow of his luxuriant hair, which is parted on the left. Lieschen understands what he says; that has long been beyond dispute. She can also understand me, whether I'm addressing her – a rare occurrence – or simply delivering one of those mumbled monologues in which I relapse into my mother tongue. I=Spaik have never tried to teach this foreign child, this urban abortion, my obsolescent German. I used ordinary Piddi-Piddi when making the few arrangements necessary in the early days of our life together, and Lieschen's actions demonstrated that she readily understood the city's lingua franca, even as spoken by me. I=Spaik didn't mind the fact that she seldom replied or asked me a question, nor did it ever occur to me to explore the reasons for her silence.

Lieschen was wished on me by the city. The nameless child caught my eye soon after I moved into the rag-boilers' quarter. A scrap dealer used to visit our street at irregular intervals, perhaps twice a month. He rode a heavy motorcycle, a Russian military machine converted into a three-wheeled pick-up equipped with a big wire cage for transporting recyclable material: scrap metal, bottles, paper, cast-off clothing. The elderly dealer was a Zeushene – at least, he sported that last remaining item of the Zeushene shepherd's costume, the fezlike catskin bonnet stubbornly affected by such male Zeushenes as are resident in the city. He seldom left the saddle of his machine. The local inhabitants would come out and lob their rubbish into the wire cage, then try to wheedle a few coins out of him in return. To me, being a still inquisitive foreigner, the real eye-catcher was his assistant, a girl with limbs like matchsticks. Clambering around inside the wire cage with apelike agility and clinging to the mesh by her fingers and toes, she sorted the assembled scrap and stacked it in accordance with some esoteric system.

Neither credit nor blame attaches to me for the fact that, a few months later, Lieschen left the wire cage for my roof space and acquired her name there. The old scrap dealer chose me as his successor, so to speak, by dropping dead outside my front door. He tumbled out of the saddle and landed almost at my feet, because I=Spaik had gone over to his machine for the very first time, intending to toss a few empty *zuleika* bottles into the wire cage. The dead man had probably succumbed to an internal haemorrhage, a perforated ulcer, because a surprising amount of dark blood gushed from his mouth into the roadway. The catskin bonnet had fallen off to reveal the leathery skin and bulging veins of the old man's bald pate. When I tore my eyes away from it, we – the foreign newcomer, the dead man, the quietly puttering motorcycle, and the girl in the cage – found ourselves hemmed in by local residents. It was clear from the way they were staring that only one course of action lay open to me. Having no idea what that proper course of action was, however, I should inevitably have called down their curses on my head had not Suqum made up my mind for me. Suqum, the silent, scowling baker who daily sold me his nut- and raisin-studded loaves of white bread, picked up the girl and threw her to me. I had no time to catch her, but her thin limbs clamped themselves around my body with instinctive assurance. I staggered backwards, but some vigorous shoves from behind prevented me from falling over. After that, my neighbours set to work on the dead man's possessions. His wares were re-sorted and stowed in plastic bags. Even the motorcycle was dismantled into its principal components and borne away. Finally, the baker and one of his apprentices wrapped the Zeushene's corpse in a plastic sheet, together with his catskin bonnet, and dragged the bundle into the shelter of a nearby courtyard.

German Fun is over. Heinz left his fly buttons alone. The Bureau had no message for me, unlike my pneumatic post correspondent. But for his anonymous communication, I= Spaik would not know that my body must be conveyed to a place of safety. He alone has informed me that my successor cannot take over my post until he has relieved the city of my mouth odour.

Lieschen is staring at the plastic sponge bag, which I'm still holding. At length she takes it from my lap and examines it from every angle. She seems to like the floral pattern on its grimy surface. Her look of enquiry asks me what it's called. My voice, grown hoarse from hours of disuse, croaks the correct appellation. I=Spaik feel sure I used to call such a receptacle a sponge bag, and I assume that people at home still call it that when required to do so. Lieschen silently repeats the words, mouthing them with exaggerated care as she always does when memorizing some new addition to her vocabulary. Then, without warning, she empties the contents of the sponge bag – the shaving things

I've just packed – on to the seat of the television chair between us. She regards the razor, shaving brush, stub end of soap and aftershave with a sullen expression, then sweeps them on to the floor with one violent gesture. Briskly swinging her legs off the chair, she brings the heel of her left orthopaedic boot down, with obvious intent, on my bottle of aftershave. In a trice, the room is filled with a scent whose intensity, whose synthetic pungency, I never notice in the daily course of events. Lieschen tramples the splintered glass with her hobnailed boots, and my shaving things, too, disintegrate under her aimed blows. The grimy sponge bag she hurls in my face together with a single swear word, a profanity I haven't heard for ages, presumably because no occasion to use it has ever arisen, either in Heinz's jocular, rudimentary German patter, or in one of *German Fun*'s commercials, or in the crass singsong of my own soliloquies.

8 Trust

I=Spaik am on my way. Lieschen has sent me off across the roofs. No one can see me up here. No one would willingly set foot on the blistering rooftops at noon, not even one of the city's leather-pawed cats or horny-clawed hens. Even the wooden shingles are so hot that I=Spaik venture to touch them only briefly with my fingertips when ascending a slope. As for the thin tiles cut from the pink slate of the Northern Range, let alone the lead sheets of which irregular pieces are skilfully hammered together to cover the roofs of blue clay buildings, they would burn my hand if it rested on them even for a moment.

Even Lieschen's quarters were unbearably hot. I=Spaik had forgotten how poorly insulated the roof space is. The sweat that erupted from my pores in Lieschen's domain had a strange, syrupy consistency. The tarlike substance with which the shingles are sealed from inside was blowing little bubbles and gave off a simultaneously mineral and ethereal smell. It seemed miraculous that something so desiccated could still smell so strongly. As soon as we had climbed the ladder in turn, Lieschen sat down in front of her whispering television set and left me to inspect her quarters. I=Spaik crawled around on all fours, keeping within range of the glow from the screen. The party walls, which begin in the cellar and extend upwards for two storeys, end at my ceiling. The shingled roof is supported by the outer walls and a number of wooden posts that run the length of the roof space like rows of columns. Beside one of these posts I sighted Lieschen's latrine. It had never occurred to me to wonder how the girl relieved herself up there. The small tin bucket was secured to one of the posts with string to guard against accidental spillage, and a plastic bag of sawdust served to absorb liquid and unpleasant odours. Lieschen had threaded her lavatory paper on a piece of string and hung it on a nail, possibly in imitation of my own practice downstairs.

Now, on an ancient wooden roof that groans like an animal at every step I take, my eye falls on a section of street, the mouth of the alleyway that leads to the video bazaar. That means I'm halfway there. Lieschen exhorted me to make my way across the roofs to Axom in three coherent German sentences. I=Spaik must therefore get used to the idea that she not only understands German but can speak it as well. I'd always known that she wasn't inhibited from speaking fluently by any physical defect. Whenever we went out together, either to the neighbouring vegetable market, or to the video bazaar, or to Axom's workshop, she spoke Piddi-Piddi extremely tersely and in a sharp, barking voice. Hardly a word crossed her lips at home, but some mornings, when half-awake after a few hours' sleep, I would hear, issuing from the open hatchway to her roof space, droning, humming sounds so deep and resonant that they seemed incompatible with the girl's scrawny frame.

Axom's house, a narrow building of grey brick, is now in sight. I still have four roofs to cross, all of them sloping towards the street. Axom has been our shoemaker ever since Lieschen was thrown at me. The first time we visited his workshop – Lieschen was clinging to my back like a monkey – I mistook him for a Greek, perhaps because many of the city's humbler craftsmen are of Hellenic stock. But Axom rejected my supposition and claimed that his family was descended from one of the warlike mountain tribes that used to prey on the city's trade routes. Highway robbery by these tribal gangs did not cease until the occupying power, at the height of its authority, put an end to it by dropping fragmentation and gas bombs on their mountain villages. Some of the surviving inhabitants, either demoralized or reduced to wholly clandestine resistance, migrated to the city and settled there as day labourers, garbage collectors, alteration tailors, and shoemakers.

Axom is a good shoemaker. Doc Zinally, who recommended him to us, erred on the side of understatement. The orthopaedic boots of which Axom has already made Lieschen more than a dozen pairs are not only ugly but strangely disparate. No one pair resembles another. The left boot never matches the right, and the dyed black leather always displays bizarre features: a strip of matted fur on the instep, a lone disk of rubber on the sole, an old scrap of wood stitched into the heel reinforcement for no discernible reason. I must have looked dubious and mistrustful when Axom laboriously manoeuvred Lieschen's feet into her very first pair of boots. The instep and toes of each foot were variously misshapen – not deformed or mutilated, but distorted by reason of long, unnatural use when clambering around inside the cage. The skin was horny, not only on the sole, and the toes displayed awe-inspiring mobility when superposed in a series of different positions. Axom took a good hour to insert Lieschen's feet in her first boots and do up their complicated system of laces, which he carefully tightened, loosened, and tightened once more. It was impossible to tell whether or not Lieschen found this lengthy procedure painful, but Axom cursed and swore in a way that verged on the offensive. He drew up three-legged stools of varying height to enable him to tackle the foot and boot from strange angles. When his hands proved insufficient to do up the laces on their own, as they often did, he would place his slipper on one of the taut leather thongs or tug at them with his teeth while his fat fingers squeezed and kneaded the leather. Although fittings have become easier since then, Lieschen is still incapable of changing her orthopaedic boots by herself. She continues to wear the same pair, day and night, until she needs the next size up.

Axom is expensive – exorbitantly so, some might say, because he has always, from the outset, insisted on being paid half his fee in hard currency. On Doc Zinally's advice we also keep him sweet with small gifts, mainly pornographic films of Indian origin, which Lieschen buys from the video bazaar in bargain packs of a dozen. Our shoemaker is also partial to cans of gourmet food from distant lands, because he likes the foreign labels with their incomprehensible inscriptions. Once, when we forgot to bring him a present of this kind, he sent us away on some flimsy pretext and Lieschen had to wait days for her next pair of boots, which were a mere three millimetres bigger.

To get to Axom's roof, I=Spaik have to leap across a narrow alleyway, a passage little wider than the average man's shoulders. I make it without landing on my hands. Axom's roof is sheathed in lead. My synthetic rubber soles detach themselves from the hot sheets of metal with a repulsive sucking sound. The skylight is improvised out of an old car door. I look down through it, straight into Axom's workshop. In addition to shoes and boots, Axom makes saddles and harness, holsters, and the ornamental quirts which many young men wear in their belts or looped to their wrists. He also does a small illegal trade in used handguns. Axom's current stock reposes on some shelves just inside the door. More than once during Lieschen's fittings, I have seen prospective buyers enter, utter a few words of greeting, and turn to the said shelves without more ado. The dozen-odd shoeboxes contain a modest selection of pistols, mostly of Italian or East European manufacture, wrapped in tissue paper and clean rags. The last time I looked through them I was struck by only one ballistic rarity, a very old but very well-maintained English revolver.

These guns were Lieschen's reason for sending me here: she told me, in her crystalline German, to buy a 'shooting iron' from Axom. If the little girl takes that tone with me these days, it's my own fault. I made the mistake from which all else flowed at an early stage, on the second or third day after Suqum threw her to me. We'd started to clean out the roof space, and the job became arduous and tedious once we set about removing the older, rock-hard layers of chicken shit. I=Spaik had taken a vacuum flask of Zuleika-Cola up to the attic with me, but its invigorating effects were short-lived. Before long I was lolling against one of the roof posts, irrigating my throat by sucking up little mouthfuls of the cold swill through a straw. Excremental dust stung my eyes as I watched the child that had fallen to my lot chipping off petrified chicken shit with a screwdriver too big for her hands. I=Spaik saw the dust-whitened soles of her feet curl with effort as she levered it off, and several times, in a crass commentary on what I was gawping at, I uttered the words 'Busy Lizzy' – 'Fleissiges Lieschen' – in my native tongue. Although I'd spoken in a murmur little louder than the sound I made sucking at my straw, the girl stopped work and turned to stare at me. The upper third of her face, which was powdered with chicken dung, looked so immensely broad, so perfectly triangular in shape and so uniformly white, that fatuous repetition was all that could maintain some kind of reassuring relationship between it and myself. So my throat continued, to the point of painful desiccation, to bleat 'Lieschen' until that stupid, ultra-German name finally attached itself to that unfamiliar countenance.

9 Curiosity

At teatime on the Esperanza's grandiose terrace, whose small wooden columns resemble the bars of a prison cell, the hotel management welcomed us with a silver carafe of chilled *zuleika*. You knew you'd like the drink even before you sampled it. As befitted medical men travelling on behalf of an international relief agency, however, we confined ourselves to taking cautious sips and contorted our faces into an equivocally judicial expression.

After delivering his illustrated lecture, Kuhl had given us a brief look at a photograph that struck him as suspect. It had been taken years before by an Italian paparazzo who had gone prospecting in the former Egichaean quarter and the night-life district that abutted on the Goto. With an unerring nose for the charms of depravity, the Italian had concentrated on the city's foreign residents. The photograph in question was alleged to be of Spaik, which was why Kuhl felt he could not withhold it from us despite his misgivings. In the lower half of the picture, in the foreground, we made out a bare, moderately well-muscled arm, probably that of an adolescent youth. The hand was holding a small, empty glass bowl between the tips of the thumb and forefinger. The second male figure visible in the background was indistinct, although the head and upper body occupied the bulk of the picture. The man's left temple was resting against a brightly painted column. His face looked relaxed, as if he was asleep. The right eye was closed, the left was half open and seemed to be staring at the camera in a strangely imbecilic but insistent manner. Kuhl wouldn't give us the photograph. It was unlikely, he said, that it really did depict Spaik. He always allowed for worst-case scenarios – he was duty-bound to do so – but that Spaik could have changed so utterly belonged to the realm of fantasy and conjecture. We concurred. It's common knowledge that foreigners unused to the climate are tempted to consume excessive quantities of *zuleika* and medicaments, occasioning an injurious interaction that quickly renders them oedematous, but the face in the photograph had lost all its salient features, every trace of personality. There was something Mongol, almost moon-like, about it, and no aspect of its yellowish rotundity was reminiscent of the Spaik the videotape had shown us earlier.

We ordered some tea and sent for the menu. In Spaik's early days, when he himself was staying at the Esperanza, the hotel, its terrace, its huge cellar bar and microphone-infested rooms had been one big espionage market, the intelligence sluiceway of the city and, thus, of the entire region. This was where the ascertainable was stored, where it was processed with the aid of tricks old and new and pumped so full of importance that the messages flowing out to countries all over the world testified to the legendary productivity of their source. You thought at first glance that nothing much had changed. Hotel guests at the tables around us were conversing with parrotlike intensity. Their comings and goings kept the big revolving door that led to the lobby in constant, whirling motion. The terrace was also frequented by visitors from the street. One or two foppishly dressed young locals sauntered among the tables, staring at their occupants. It would doubtless have been easy to establish contact with these roving youths, but something about our manner seemed to deter them at the very last moment. At your suggestion, we deliberately refrained from smiling and strove to look like two honest Austrians soured by their labours on behalf of an international organization. In fact, two men did stop at our table in quick succession. One asked if we were interested in purchasing archaeological relics, little clay figurines of Scythian hunting and fertility goddesses that could easily be smuggled through customs. The other tried to rent us some adolescent peasant girls by the hour. Once every three months – the next consignment was due tomorrow, as it happened – the cog railway brought him fresh supplies from the valleys of the Northern Range, which were still very inaccessible.

It wasn't until the waiter had placed some dishes of regional hors d'oeuvres on our table that we were accosted by a worthy conversationalist. He made an immediate impression on us. Neither of us had ever seen a man so tall and, at the same time, so emaciated. His lilac linen jacket fitted him as tightly as if the tailor had measured each of his ribs and allowed for their protrusions by skilfully inserting extra seams. The gaunt giant introduced himself by some

polysyllabic local name and apologized in the next breath
for its incomprehensibility. His Piddi-Piddi was soft and
drawling; it sounded just like a Central European variant of
the language, you said later, if ever such a thing were to
evolve. We addressed our first acquaintance as Freddy at
his request and invited him to join us. He forbore to ask
where we hailed from and why we had come, just as we
refrained from commenting on the peculiar intonation of
his Piddi-Piddi. There followed an unforced and enter-
taining conversation, initially about the city's climate and
its disastrous effects on the health of the foreigners who
lived there.

Over his lilac jacket Freddy wore an elegant coat whose
viscose material displayed iridescent shades of pink and
beige resembling mother-of-pearl. He spread the expertly
pressed pleats to show us how amply it was cut and
advised us to wear equally voluminous clothing. Tweaking
your trouser legs, he explained that such fashionably close-
fitting garments would prevent sufficient air from circulating around our muscular thighs and jocularly but insist-
ently warned us against their potential effect on the nether
organs. All foreigners were additionally advised to frequent
a traditional steam bath. The proverbial virility of the local
males was attributable in no small measure to the fact that
they spent every second or third night in such an establishment, a custom almost unaffected by changes in the local
way of life. Foreigners were barred from all the traditional
steam baths, unfortunately, and the sauna clubs of the
night-life district were, at best, travesties of the old baths
and fraught with health hazards. For that reason, not that

he needed to advertise, he recommended selected visitors like us to sample his own establishment. Freddy's Steam Bath was the only respectable alternative for foreigners of refinement. Like himself, his steam bath constituted an attempt to build a bridge between different cultures, and what, in the present state of international tension, could be more important?

We agreed with Freddy and assured him that, although we were young and fit, our own health mattered deeply to us. We would, we said, be his guests tomorrow at the latest, if not today. Then we steered the conversation to the Esperanza, a subject on which Freddy proved equally knowledgeable and informative. Although rich in tradition, the hotel had definitely lost much of its erstwhile glamour. Freddy recalled the old days with nostalgia. Only a few years ago, on this very terrace, he had seen militant devotees of Gahis strip a noted Swiss arms dealer naked and compel him, while standing on a table, to discourse on his business activities in all the languages he knew – no fewer than half a dozen of them! To the surprise of all present, the Gahists had been prevented from leaving by the Lebanese honorary consul, a construction plant importer of Zeushene extraction. This short, bald-headed individual, a keen businessman and diplomat, came storming out on to the terrace with an enormous revolver in his fist and demanded, in excellent French, the return of the Swiss victim's clothes. Afterwards, people had cracked jokes about where the intrepid consul could have hidden the big handgun under his clothing. He fired three thunderous shots in the air and gave the Gahists five seconds in which to see reason. One of them had already cocked an Israeli sub-machine gun and was holding it in readiness behind the back of one of his white-robed confederates. The short-barrelled weapon, which had a wide arc of fire, would have wreaked carnage among the hotel guests and the many curious spectators who were now thronging the terrace. Fortunately for all present, however, and also for the hot-tempered consul, the manageress of the Esperanza was on the spot. A woman of unrivalled courage and, at that time, physical strength, Madame Haruri – here Freddy broke off and raised his glass to the said lady – caught hold of the little man from behind, hefted him off the ground, and clamped his gun arm so tightly to his side that all he could have shot was his patent leather shoes.

Freddy aimed his forefinger at the roof of the hotel. The Esperanza was built in the bombastic style of the former occupying power. Every conceivable historical feature of the local architecture – ornaments, barley-sugar columns, balconies, oriels – had been misused with unbridled plagiaristic greed in order to lend the concrete colossus a façade that simulated variety and depth. Madame Haruri still resided on high, where the stone-shingled roof was interrupted by a row of glassed-in balconies, but no one had seen her in public, either in the hotel or elsewhere, for the last two years. It was alleged that she had long been confined to a wheelchair, her face contorted by the involuntary spasms typical of *mau*. This rumour had provoked horrified speculation, and not only among the Esperanza's patrons, because experience had hitherto shown that foreigners alone succumbed to the disease and its repulsive symptoms, and no one had doubted that Madame Haruri was a native immune to that regional virus.

Freddy heaved a deep, lingering sigh. For the first time since we had invited him to do so, he helped himself. Taking a vine-leaf roll stuffed with nut purée between his lips, he thrust it halfway into his mouth. Instead of biting some off, however, he discreetly licked and sucked it. Then, holding it up to his eyes almost intact, he regarded it thoughtfully and repeated the procedure twice more before depositing it on the edge of his plate, well away from the other hors d'oeuvres, as if reserving it for future consumption.

10 Providence

I=Spaik almost collided with Freddy's lanky figure in the street. He was coming down the steps of the Esperanza's terrace into Freedom of Speech Boulevard. His coat swung forward as his storklike legs took the last two steps at a single stride. Then he turned away, and I=Spaik remained invisible to him, half hidden by a news-vendor's kiosk. I had encountered Freddy outside his steam bath only once over the years, and that was when we bumped into each other at the door of Doc Zinally's waiting room. Freddy was emerging from the surgery, I was going in, and a malign fate ordained that the two of us should simultaneously grasp the doorhandle as patients – in other words, more naked than we'd ever been in the steam bath.

Although our near miss just now strikes me as a good omen, my heart is still beating wildly under my shirt and skin. I've also broken out in a sweat. With one shoulder propped against the kiosk, I=Spaik get out my pillbox. My fingertips fasten on two, then three, then four of the colourful tablets. They will have to negotiate my gullet dry, because the hip flask Lieschen filled with *zuleika* for my mountaineering trip to Axom and hung round my neck on a string is empty: I drained it in the doorway of his workshop before continuing on my way through the streets.

I=Spaik left Axom empty-handed. When I expressed a wish to buy a handgun in faltering Piddi-Piddi, Axom, who was seated at his last, indicated the shelves beside the door with his cobbler's hammer. I opened one shoebox after the other, vainly rummaged around in tissue paper and soft rags, and neatly shut each box before reaching for the next. Behind me, Axom was hammering away at a boot sole. Just as I=Spaik was endeavouring to shove the last shoebox, which had proved to be as empty as all the rest, back into place on the top shelf with my fingertips, the shoemaker gave a sudden bellow of laughter and, in the harsh, guttural intonation of a native of the mountains, called out the word with which the market supervisors close the vegetable and cattle markets at nightfall. It means 'sold out' in the sense that anyone still wishing to buy something has turned up too late.

Although the rear of the news-stand is completely plastered with periodicals, the stallholder has spotted me hovering there. He comes out from behind his counter and peremptorily brandishes a handful of foreign newspapers under my nose. I=Spaik buy an Italian sports journal. Clamped beneath my arm, the garish pink paper will make it easier for me to ascend the Esperanza's terrace. Ever since I moved out of the South Oriel Suite – my first grave infringement of foreign service regulations – I=Spaik have withdrawn myself, my knowledge and my desire for knowledge from the orbit of the Esperanza's traffic in information. Not even the terrace, which is readily accessible from the boulevard and keeps washing new arrivals and long-time expatriates over its extremities like a prospector panning for gold, has since been permitted to expose me to enquiring eyes.

I=Spaik have not, until now, shunned the hotel and all other overly public places for my personal safety's sake. I was not threatened by any dangers that had to be guarded against by adopting such rules of behaviour. None of the three local secret services alarms me, not even the notorious Special Section 9 of the People's Militia, which regularly, on obscure pretexts, picks up inebriated foreigners and subjects them to special treatment of a humiliating nature. I= Spaik am in possession of the Blue Permanent Visa stamped by the National Liberation Council and the International Control Authority. No foreigner could have more in the way of protection. Welded into laminated plastic, the blue card is suspended from my waist on an elastic nylon cord unbreakable by muscle power alone. Thus equipped, I= Spaik have withstood three body searches, the first at the Esperanza itself, when the terrace was stormed by Gahists. On that occasion a Swiss businessman found his precious passport and his excellent command of languages more of a liability than an asset. Stark naked and glistening with cold sweat, he was made to stand on one of the veranda tables. Only Madame Haruri, whom my eyes have been privileged to see in full possession of her physical strength, preserved him and many of the others present – myself included, perhaps – from a worse fate.

Axom explained why he didn't have a single hand-gun left in stock. Tomorrow, he told me, was the ninth anniversary of the Great Gahis's death. Nine was the magic number of his work. His sermons and canticles were divided into nine parts and had always been sold on as many video cassettes, even though there were now tapes of sufficient duration to have enabled them all to be transferred to one alone. Every local inhabitant – even the Zeushenes in the accumulated heat of their catskin bonnets – was smart enough to grasp what prophecies were associated with the ninth anniversary of Gahis's demise. Even my own poor, foreigner's powers of anticipation must convey some inkling of them despite the local proverb: 'Westerners hammer the future into their children's heads like a rusty nail.' That was why he, Axom, would tell me where a gun was still to be had, now that the locals had snapped up the rest.

So I=Spaik am standing outside the Esperanza on Axom's advice. He told me of a relative who, like himself, deals in handguns, using a long dialect word whose numerous components seemed to indicate the degree of kinship between them. I was astonished when he mentioned this other arms dealer's name because it turned out that I knew him: the person he advised me to contact was old Lui.

Now that I=Spaik am climbing the steps of the Esperanza's terrace, armed only with an Italian sports journal, I find it easy enough to recollect the floor waiter in question: bald and stooping, almost hump-backed, bent over a gilt serving trolley in an attitude of boundless, almost aggressive servility. Lui was in charge of the room-service and cleaning staff on the floor that terminated in my South Oriel

Suite. He had since retired, Axom told me. Rendered unfit
for work by an abraded, wafer-thin spinal disc, he had been
privileged after half a century's service to move into one of
the few attic rooms reserved for Esperanza pensioners. Up
there, with nothing between himself and Madame Haruri's
penthouse but a substantial fire wall, old Lui led a pain-
racked existence. He earned his keep and the electricity he
consumed, for which the hotel made him pay, by performing odd jobs.

One foot on the bottom step, I=Spaik pause to survey the
terrace. With knee-trembling nostalgia, my eyes come to
rest on the table at which, as a new arrival, I used to take
my hotel meals. It is now in the possession of two foreigners. Seated shoulder to shoulder, far closer together
than is our custom, these youthful West or Central Europeans are occupying the position of my bygone self. A
waiter is clearing away some silver hors d'oeuvres dishes.
They are almost empty. All the young fellows have left is
a single vine-leaf roll. We foreigners are despised for our
gluttony, to which even I, a long-time resident, still
succumb from time to time. To quote one of the city's prov-
erbs: 'What the pig spurns, the foreigner wolfs.' Half
attracted, half repelled, I cannot tear my eyes away from the
youngsters. One of them is whispering to the other, his lips
in contact with his companion's ear. Whatever he's saying,
it clearly has to be instilled into the auditory canal with an
admixture of moist breath. Now he thrusts the tip of his
tongue into the hollow of the ear, once, twice, three times. I
know of no European language whose articulation requires
the tongue to emerge so far from the shelter of the teeth.

Perhaps the young men are speaking Piddi-Piddi. When we foreigners are in the preliminary stage of its assimilation, we have a tendency to exaggerate its mouth movements. I= Spaik have observed a whole series of beginners shoot out their tongues and involuntarily bare their teeth.

The couple have sensed me watching them. They glance over at me simultaneously. Their tanned faces beam in a friendly, homely fashion, their gaze holds me fast. Now, the two smilers raise their hands in gestures of which one is a strange mirror image of the other. Quite unmistakably, their twin figures are signalling to me to join them at my old table.

11 Gaiety

A very down-at-heel foreigner, an Italian whom we beckoned over to our table, did not, unfortunately, feel like joining us. The unkempt, ill-smelling fellow claimed to have a prior appointment in the hotel's cellar bar. Long-time residents of his type, whose squalid appearance clearly shows how far they have succumbed to the city's influence, are reputed to be talkative and trustworthy informants. Spaik said as much in his earliest, correctly drafted reports, and Freddy, the man who has so obligingly invited us to patronize his steam bath, expressed himself in similar terms. But it suited you quite well that the ageing, unprepossessing fellow hadn't joined us. Still savouring our meal, we were looking forward to a *zuleika* coffee and some of the city's celebrated sweet-and-salt pastries. The taste of those specialities would certainly not have been enhanced by the squalid Italian's acrid, goatlike body odour.

The *zuleika* coffee proved to be an incomparably harmonious blend of sweetish and bitter aromas, and the pastries that accompanied it fulfilled our high expectations. You promptly ordered some more, and with them the waiter brought the forms of which the desk clerk had told us this morning. They were sheets folded in four, and one of them, when opened out, covered almost the entire table-top. Kuhl had warned us that we might be subjected to bureaucratic harassment. International supervisory agencies, multitudinous government ministries, obscure local authorities – all such office-holders jealously competed for the most trivial prerogatives and special powers. What confronted us was a decree jointly promulgated by Immigration Control and the People's Ministry of Health. All foreigners had to undergo a medical examination within forty-eight hours of their arrival in the city, the ostensible purpose of this compulsory measure being to intercept travellers infected with *mau*.

We knew about *mau*. Spaik's controller had touched on this strange phenomenon in his briefing. The incidence of the disease is still confined to the city and its surrounding districts, and it seems that its appalling symptoms can only develop fully in foreigners from the West. Kuhl reported the view prevailing among our own medical experts, which is that the city's inhabitants are immune to the ancient local virus but can pass it on to unprotected travellers. In the city itself, by contrast, *mau* is accounted a venereal disease recently imported from the degenerate West. It appears that the local inhabitants are fond of boasting, especially in conversation with foreigners, that their robust and untainted bodies are resistant to the pernicious body fluids that carry the disease.

One of Spaik's reports, quoted by Kuhl, embodied a proverb current in the city: 'Better your head up a dog's anus than your nose in the pestilential stench of the west wind.' With undisguised pride, Spaik's controller pointed out that the potentially explosive international repercussions of the disease had been spotted by his agent and conveyed to the authorities at home long before the first press reports appeared. Indeed, Spaik had used the name *mau*, a medical contraction, in his very first report, although it was not officially introduced until a year later, at a symposium of the World Epidemiological Agency. We disliked the emotionalism that had suddenly and unmistakably crept into Kuhl's voice. To vaunt his protégé's intelligence-gathering prowess was a breach of every rule governing in-house communication. Smitten with the kind of embarrassment one feels on hearing an old man tell a smutty joke, we forbore to ask him any more questions about *mau*.

We studied the closely printed, almost calligraphically typeset form. The decree of the People's Ministry of Health had been translated into five European languages and Japanese. Its rendering into our good old German, which was appallingly clumsy and studded with abstruse errors, had presumably been concocted with the aid of obsolete software by someone ignorant of the language. We kept to the English version of the text. The prescribed health inspection could not, it seemed, be avoided. The folded sheet gave details of the municipal out-patients' departments at which the examination could be conducted, together with an alphabetical list of qualified physicians with surgeries of their own. You ran your fingertip down the column of minuscule print and paused at a name whose syllabic sequence seemed to denote a Western origin: Lynch Zinally. Another point in Dr Zinally's favour was the location of his surgery, which was situated in Freedom of Speech Boulevard. Almost all the other addresses were the customary local abbreviations, which can comprise as many as ten letters and numerals. These were not just encoded street names, we knew, but a positional system governed by its own logic. It dates from the early heyday of Gahism, when the sect was flourishing underground, and is proudly – because of its esoteric nature – attributed to the Great Gahis himself. Even mediocre taxi drivers have to know over a hundred such abbreviations by heart and be capable of converting them into routes and destinations. In everyday life, townsfolk make do with the names of resident families, conspicuous buildings, or events whose memory still clings to the places where they occurred. Street names dating from the foreign occupation are strictly taboo, however, and Kuhl strongly advised us not to use them when dealing with the local townsfolk.

According to Kuhl, not even the Bureau possesses a serviceable map of the city. Existing maps, which hail from prerevolutionary times, are regarded as unreliable. The occupying power had not shrunk from deleting streets whose demolition was envisaged by its grandiose five-year plans and substituting the phantom avenues that would traverse its projected redevelopments. Kuhl regretted that the evaluation of satellite photographs was still at a preliminary stage, their quality being impaired by the dome of smog surmounting the urban area and the heavy overcast between the sea and the mountains. When Kuhl illustrated the relative positions of the city's main districts with the aid of a diagram, you instantly recognized the curious conformation of Freedom of Speech Boulevard as something prescribed by nature. Like a noose, its southern end encloses the Ghetto of the Great Prophecy, known in the urban dialects and in Piddi-Piddi as the Goto. It has been out of bounds to foreigners ever since the occupying power withdrew. In a seductively paradoxical way, however, the parallel streets between the boulevard and the Goto have become home to brothels, dance halls and sauna clubs. This night-life mecca forms a narrow but miles-long buffer zone between the city's main arteries and the forbidden quarter. The Goto, the city's oldest coherent architectural complex, covers three hills. Their dense agglomeration of multi-storeyed but incredibly narrow blue clay buildings of the medieval period would be a world-class tourist attraction if visitors from abroad could be admitted and accommodated there.

You intimated that it was time to go. The walk to Dr Lynch Zinally's surgery would be our first reconnaissance of the city. We had decided to take our time – in fact we even treated ourselves to a stroll along the boulevard in the wrong direction. The Bureau had given us three days and nights in which to find Spaik and eliminate the problem associated with his name. We were feeling refreshed. Your smile was relaxed, your step springy. We became as light-hearted as we always are when borne along on the wings of an assignment, and the world we were entering seemed to exhale a wind filled with promise.

12 Refreshment

The Esperanza, which I=Spaik have entered sodden with sweat and knees atremble, seems to bear me no grudge. Like a foster mother finally appeased by the excessive number of her charges, the hotel has readmitted its long-lost guest. Leaving the terrace and the two foreigners seated at my former table, I=Spaik have ventured as far as the cellar bar. Its brownish twilight hasn't changed over the years; if anything, it has become a shade darker. I thread my way between the serried, still deserted tables, and no sooner are my hands resting on the brass rim of the counter, thumbs linked just as in the old days, than a promising contact presents itself: the door behind the counter is ajar, enabling me to see into a small kitchen. A young black man is cutting lemons, the extremely sour local kind, into cocktail slices. He senses my gaze, looks up and sees me, and his face twists into a grimace of recognition. Although he probably means me to interpret his baring of the teeth as a surprised smile, it's more as if he's trying to threaten me, the apparition from the past, in impotent panic.

No. 243's alarm and his lingering look of fear send a powerful current of strength surging through me. Quietly, using his old number, I=Spaik summon the youth to join me

78

at the counter. By obeying, he dispels my last remaining doubts: he's the gifted linguist who disappeared from Freddy's Steam Bath overnight. This is the first time I've ever set eyes on a former houseboy in his life after Freddy. I=Spaik tell him what I want of him, and he at once, with nervous alacrity, devises a means of fulfilling my request. We leave the bar by way of the kitchen and board an old-fashioned service lift, which sets off almost without a sound. In the lift cage, 243 has to endure being scrutinized by me at very close range. The young man has acquired a remarkably powerful physique in the service of the hotel. His neck muscles strain against the collar of his uniform tunic, his shoulders are broader and his buttocks less pronounced than I remember. Although he's now too old for my taste, I find his fearful, tremulous gaze delightfully rejuvenating.

On the top floor we're greeted by a windowless corridor illuminated by low-wattage bulbs suspended from the ceiling at long intervals. My guide pauses outside one of the low doors and indicates the handle. My question whether I should give his regards to Freddy hits him smack in the sweating face. Gripping my right hand two-handed, he entreats me in a whisper to tell no one, neither Freddy nor Axom nor Lui, that he has guided me to this door. Then, having tongue-kissed my hand, he hurries off down the corridor without a backward glance.

My visit to Axom's relative – my reunion with old Lui – was a brief one. It took me three steps forward to enter the cramped little room and three steps backward to regain the corridor in double-quick time. My eyes lingered on old

Lui's face until the door hid it from view. Such spectacles are rare indeed. Victims of *mau* waste away slowly. Their death throes take place in seclusion, usually in one of the cheap boarding houses at the rear of the night-life district. Lui is my second victim of *mau*. The first *mau*-disfigured corpse I saw was that of the previous occupant of my little house in the rag-boilers' quarter, an Italian photojournalist. At that time, only a few weeks after my arrival in the city, *mau* still had no name. The Italian had gone to Doc Zinally for treatment, and Zinally, knowing that I was looking for somewhere to live, had told me that he was very ill and would soon have to give up his lodgings. I=Spaik went to see this fleeting acquaintance and found him in precisely the same state as old Lui. Incredible, how a victim's death throes can once more galvanize his emaciated features. A final process of muscular contraction had wrenched Lui's mouth wide open, exposing the throat and causing the tongue to protrude, stiff and erect as a free-standing column. In this rigid state, which is typical of all *mau* deaths, Lui's old face was recognizable by one peripheral feature alone: the ears, which possess no musculature and cannot be deformed by the disease. I=Spaik had caught a last glimpse of Lui's big and exceptionally ugly ears with their hairy, misshapen lobes, a sight that continues to fill me with regret. It would, after all, have been so easy to whisper my desire for a gun into the former floor waiter's enormous auricles.

Lui's corpse was not entirely fresh. Even without examining it by touch, I could tell that it was cold. The soul – the last, hot, intestinal wind of the expiring body, as the Great

Gahis allegedly calls it in one of his nine canticles – had undoubtedly left old Lui hours before. As for the Italian photographer, he may have lain dead for three or four days in the bed that is now my own. His tongue, frozen by *mau*-induced spasms into a long, vertical protrusion, had been deeply fissured by desiccation; the gums, visible as far as the uvula, had the dark sheen of the fillets of smoked perch that are sandwiched between two halves of a bun and sold everywhere as a snack. Lifeless flesh is quickly dehydrated by the city's dry heat. The Italian might well have continued to lie there in his lodgings with no sign of decay. The parchmentlike consistency of his skin and the dull, glazed surface of his eyeballs suggested that he was steadily becoming mummified.

The owner of the little rag-boiler's house, a goat's-meat and donkey-meat butcher from the quarter's southern outskirts, accepted me as a tenant provided I paid a year's rent in advance and discreetly disposed of the Italian's body. Freddy recommended a Cyrenian undertaker who was prepared, on certain conditions, to remove dead foreigners from the city and cremate them at a bonemeal plant downriver. The undertaker's men turned up punctually at nightfall but refused, in view of the way he was lying, to take hold of the dead man and lift him into the coffin. I= Spaik had first to stow him in a plastic body bag. Employing a minimum of words and gestures, the two pallbearers indicated that the corpse's fingers must be broken to loosen their grip on his ankles. They found it harder to explain how to eliminate the curvature of the torso, which was bent like a bow. In the end, one of them played the dead man while the other mounted his jutting backside to illustrate how the corpse's hip joints and lumbar vertebrae could be snapped back into a tolerably flat position by jumping up and down on them with the full weight of one's body. I=Spaik did my best, but when the dead man was more or less straightened out and wrapped in black plastic sheeting, I discovered that the Cyrenian corpse recyclers had found some excuse to decamp with the money I'd already handed them.

Lui's death has spoilt my chances of obtaining a gun. On the other hand, the floor waiter's corpse proves that a native has died of *mau*, and that I find refreshing. The desire to tell Doc Zinally about it wells up inside me, filling me with malicious and pleasurable anticipation. I=Spaik produce my pillbox and flip back the lid, stir the contents with my thumb. My fingertips happen upon a small, oval capsule divided into two halves, one sky-blue and the other white. It must be a new addition to Doc Zinally's assortment, whose composition he varies gradually and with care. I=Spaik am familiar with some of the tablets from my very earliest weeks in the city, when my ailments were being unsuccessfully treated by other physicians. I've long forgotten the names of those drugs, but the shape and colour of certain pills, capsules, and dragées are so distinctive that they look conspicuous even among the motley selection customarily prescribed by Doc Zinally for us, his grateful patients.

I put the pillbox to my ear and shake it awhile – shake it until my tongue and gums have sucked the new capsule soft. It tastes of synthetic vanilla: I=Spaik recognize this staple flavour – this product of good old German scientific ingenuity – and relish its chemical, unnatural intensity. Doc Zinally is an American expatriate and patriot. Hanging in his surgery are historic photographs of the Civil War, which, as Zinally phrases it, repaired the rents in the star-spangled banner with bloodstained thread. Once a month, when I=Spaik lie naked on his padded leather couch and submit to the curious ritual of the health check, there hangs on my left a photograph showing an American negro in the uniform of the Northern States. He has deposited the bullet-riddled corpse of a white comrade on a tarpaulin and is hauling it away from the battlefield. This photograph has puzzled me ever since I=Spaik became Doc Zinally's patient. Zinally is an ethnologist, and anyone wishing to benefit from his medical expertise must endure his tirades on the relative superiority or inferiority of nations and ethnic groups. Whenever my head reposes on the couch in his surgery, he proceeds to palpate my skull and deliver dark prophecies about the obscure miscegenation of the Teutonic tribes. Zinally does not exclude himself from his besetting doubts about racial purity. The arthritis in his hands, which compelled him to abandon a surgeon's career at an early stage, he attributes to Jewish juices on the paternal side of his family tree.

The pillbox gives a hollow rattle: my stock of tablets is running low. I=Spaik must go to Zinally's and get a fresh batch of his house mixture. Hanging in the waiting room is a huge glass sphere filled with the current assortment of pills, and mounted beneath it is the mechanical section of the automat: a rusty metal cube provided with a coin slot, a clumsy dispenser, and a delivery tube. Patients can obtain the requisite coin in Zinally's consulting room. This is a worn silver dollar for which we presently have to pay our doctor three of the orange five-hundreds adorned with Gahis's portrait. My very first attempt to extract my prescribed ration from the machine ended in disaster: I failed to notice the absence of a cup beneath the pill dispenser, so my tablets, capsules, and dragées went rolling across the waiting-room floor. I=Spaik crawled around for quite a while, retrieving them from between the feet of long-standing patients who had simply sat there in silence, not deigning to warn a newcomer like me. And if, today, some other first-timer were to walk up to the glass sphere with the silver dollar between his thumb and forefinger, my initiated self would sit there among the other initiates just as mutely, making no effort to save him from a similar misfortune.

13 Lethargy

You were the first to take the hand Dr Lynch Zinally extended in welcome. He engulfed your fingers in a muscular, hairy paw. Its grip was dry and hard, and he did not relax it until he had drawn each of us a little closer and, as though already forming a diagnosis, fixed us with his bright, stone-grey eyes. Having introduced ourselves by name and profession, we waited for Dr Zinally to enquire the purpose of our visit, but he was loath to simulate collegial interest. He was clearly as indifferent to the work of the International Child Relief Agency as he was to the intentions and opinions of a brace of Austrian ophthalmologists. He had not yet heard of the official decree requiring all foreigners to be examined for *mau*. Shaking his head, he read the folded sheet we laid before him and quoted a local proverb used by Freddy in another context: 'In the sultan's palace, eunuchs have to bow down even before the farts of their sleeping sovereign.' Then he instructed us to undress, and before long we were sitting side by side on a leather couch, submitting with spuriously earnest faces to a variety of strange manipulations.

The doctor began by examining our skulls with his huge hands. Strong and supple, they ran their fingers over each of our occiputs in turn, then carefully palpated our temples, cheekbones and jaws. At the same time, as if to prevent us from becoming bored, he discoursed on *mau*. Zinally ventured to say he was one of the first to detect the beginnings of the present epidemic. A patient of his, an Italian photojournalist who had spent his summers in the city for years and had made a substantial contribution to the international renown of its artistic smart set, had come to the surgery suffering from the peculiar symptoms of the disease in its early stages. *Mau* always manifested itself first in the right-hand half of the body, mostly with minimal symptoms in the extremities. The little toe of the right foot felt cold to the touch, or the tip of the little finger of the right hand went numb for increasing periods and ended by becoming totally insensitive. At the same time, the mobility of the left eyeball displayed slight malfunctions such as an involuntary, almost imperceptible squint, a tendency to twitch, or an occasional but ultimately persistent droop of the lid – limited defects that left the patient almost unimpaired but were, taken together, indicative of a serious disturbance of the nervous system.

When you questioned Zinally about the course and duration of the epidemic, he deplored the inadequacy of the statistical records relating to those who had contracted the disease and/or died of it. In contrast to the prevailing view, he felt sure that this was not the first time it had been as rife. Older local doctors, who had worked for the occupying power, told of two epidemics antedating the present one. At the behest of the authorities, a secret documentation centre had been set up in the records office of the central hospital. Its primitive card index had at least succeeded in demonstrating features common to various cases and the failure of the treatments attempted. When a quirk of fate decreed that the city's military governor and his successor should both die, smitten with identical convulsions, in the same year, photographs were taken of the dead men. All relevant documents were stamped with a number intended to signalize their importance and confidentiality, and eventually, just before the revolution, the whole of the documentation was removed from the central hospital's archive and transferred to the Palace of People's Security. This building, which housed the secret service, the military police and the regional television centre, was subsequently, during the so-called Violet Days, stormed by the Gahists. The head of the secret service belonged to an old city family. Abandoned by the troops of the occupying power, he barricaded himself on the upper floors of the building with some local loyalists. It was only after three days of hand-to-hand, office-to-office fighting that his corpse, adorned with a garland of white violets, was hurled from the roof of the Palace of People's Security and, to the exultant cheers of the mob, came crashing down on the files of his now defunct organization, which littered the street below.

Dr Zinally knelt at our feet, breathing heavily. He twisted the toes and massaged the soles, ostensibly to test certain reflexes. We asked how many current cases of *mau* there were among foreigners resident in the city, but he brushed the question aside with an angry grunt. Although the People's Ministry of Health insisted that doctors give

immediate notice of any patient suspected of having contracted the disease, the information it devoured was never
released in any form, not even as an ordinary global stat-
istic. Ever since international health organizations and big
supraregional satellite networks had discovered the repulsive nature of the disease and evolved a wonderfully
memorable name for it, said Zinally, the authorities' attitude had vacillated between two conditions reminiscent of
mau in its terminal stages: the tetanic and the paralytic. He
himself had only one acute case under treatment at the
present time, as luck would have it, but quite a few of his
patients were chronically susceptible to local infections, and
there were many indications that *mau* could develop only
when there was a certain measure of constitutional impair-
ment. The Italian photographer, for example, had been a
very tough fellow, an enthusiastic cyclist who could often
be seen pedalling his racing bike up the steepest alleyways
in the Old City. He was well on the way to becoming a local
character, a status foreigners very seldom attained, when an
unhappy love affair with an indigenous waitress debili-
tated him mentally and enabled *mau* to triumph.

Zinally took some blood samples from us – samples of a
size we found astonishing. When you enquired the reason,
he told us that he was obliged, when examining foreigners
for the first time, to use them as blood donors. In the last
six months, hospitals had begun to install separate storage
facilities for foreigners because the allegedly pure blood of
native donors was to be reserved for their own kind. This
measure was probably attributable to pressure from one of
the many post-Gahist underground groups. The belief in

purity cherished by this sect, or by the obscure successor organizations into which it had disintegrated, was bearing fruit of an increasingly bizarre kind – a regrettable development, said Zinally, since the magnum opus of the Great Gahis himself, above all *The Bleating of the Ram*, his third canticle, had come close to being a well-founded racial theory in the Darwinian mould.

Dr Zinally urged us to acquire these canticles. The nine video cassettes on which the poet and prophet of the revolution intoned his visionary narrative poems were, he said, the finest souvenir the city had to offer its visitors. There was a version subtitled in Piddi-Piddi – a makeshift translation, to be sure, but that which the urban lingua franca could not impart was aurally and visually conveyed by Gahis's wonderfully melodramatic delivery. We should not on any account lend an ear to the dubbed version that continued to cause trouble in sundry foreign television programmes. On the strength of having a Cyrenian grandfather who hailed from the city, a Hollywood veteran had been presumptuous enough to dub the Great Gahis in his own voice. This outrageously garbled version of the nine canticles was still causing a lot of bad blood. The old film actor, three times an Oscar-winner, had only just escaped mutilation by unknown assailants who cut off half his investment adviser's tongue by mistake. Masked Gahists had handed this trophy to reporters from the local television station only two days later, together with an ominous declaration concerning the ninth anniversary of the Prophet's death, which, as Zinally felt sure we knew, would be celebrated tomorrow.

Having promised to buy the relevant tapes in the video bazaar before the day was out, we obediently sipped the bitter coffee Dr Zinally had brewed us to stimulate our circulation, which was sluggish from loss of blood. The time had come to broach our personal request. In a wealth of detail, you told Zinally about a local businessman, a friend of your father's, whose most recent sign of life had been a postcard from the city depicting the Blue Gate of Prophecy. Your father had often pondered on this greeting from afar and wished he could thank the sender. It was a touchingly plausible fiction of yours, and you refrained from mentioning Spaik's name until the single syllable transfixed Zinally like a baited hook. Taken by surprise, he made no attempt to deny all knowledge of Spaik. Yes, he said, he had indeed come across a foreigner by that unusual name – a German. He had treated the man for the usual acclimatization problems some years ago, but had no idea of his present whereabouts. His index card must be somewhere among the records in the basement. The results of our blood tests would be through tomorrow afternoon. He would look out Herr Spaik's card for us before then, though he doubted if it would tell us much.

We smiled at him gratefully. Fortune had favoured us once more. We watched Zinally pick up our own index cards, irresolutely turn them over in his hands a couple of times, then drop them on the desk. The sight of his fear was immensely gratifying. He flared his nostrils – his nose was red and coarse-pored – as if taking our scent. In Corsica you had read aloud to us from an American scientific journal. The article in question described how the largest primates behave when first confronted in their native rain forests by their human counterparts. Like those forest-dwelling gorillas, Dr Zinally seemed to scent the superior aptitudes of another species.

Back outside in Freedom of Speech Boulevard you took my arm, and we walked along entwined like many of the local men, who do this without embarrassment. We were heading for the southern end of the boulevard, which encircles the Ghetto of the Great Prophecy. Freddy had recommended us to spend an evening at the so-called Naked Truth Club. Founded during the revolutionary period as a rendezvous for bourgeois elements of Western orientation, this establishment had mutated over the years into a kind of artists' café. Literati had dominated the club for some considerable time, so Freddy informed us, and promising youngsters gave impassioned readings there every night. Piddi-Piddi was clearly developing into a literary language. Video clips of the poets, who barked out their long narrative poems and songs in a kind of Sprech-gesang, were already finding a place in the world music specials broadcast by international music channels. The boom in indigenous folk singing had still to reach its zenith, and many foreign residents, in a curious form of self-ingratiation, had become fans of these performances.

Although darkness had fallen, we felt in no hurry. The nocturnal face of the city, too, appealed to us. Loss of blood had given you an appetite, so you towed me back and forth across the broad pavement, which was lined with street vendors' stalls and handcarts, in a hard-to-please quest for something to eat. You eventually halted in front of one particular stall, and we decided to fortify ourselves with a local snack. In the white glare of a propane gas lamp, the harshest of all forms of artificial lighting, our teeth transfixed a layer of fresh bread and sank into the greasy flesh of some small smoked fish.

14 Disgust

For the first time ever, I=Spaik, who so often travel by taxi, have taken a *vuspi*, one of the orange motor scooters that can be hailed like cabs in the city's chronically congested thoroughfares. Now, after nightfall, the beams of the *vuspis'* diode headlights weave wildly back and forth above stagnant rivers of traffic. The scooters careen across the boulevard's six lanes, perilously squeezing through the smallest gaps. When one of them threads its way in from the right, pedestrians hastily step back from the kerb because the fibreglass arms tipped with orange trafficators hang low to one side and can deliver painful blows. Astride the rear half of the seat, which is slightly raised, and compelled by the machine's abrupt toings and froings to hang on tight, the passenger clings to the driver's waist as he crouches over the handlebars. I=Spaik keep my head tilted back at an evasive angle, but whenever my youthful pilot brakes sharply my nose buries itself in his greasy locks, which reek of attar of roses.

Doc Zinally's surgery was deserted. He leaves all the doors open when he goes out. Patients who turn up in his absence, as they usually do, kill time until he reappears by sleeping, dozing, or staring at the television set, which has the sound turned down. This evening there wasn't a soul to be seen in any of the four rooms. I=Spaik opened both the consulting-room doors – I even peered into the lavatory and the tiny bedroom. Zinally has no home of his own. Being hypochondriacally concerned about his health, he spends his patientless hours at Freddy's Steam Bath or ogles the city's *jeunesse* from one of the red-upholstered booths in the Naked Truth Club. I want the *vuspi* to get me there as fast as possible. The young poets who patronize the club deal in anything potentially profitable, from egg-shaped ampoules of hashish oil to the hotel room numbers of American benefactresses and ornate daggers fashioned from cheap imported screwdrivers by the craftsmen of the tinsmiths' souk. Tonight, perhaps, a serviceable handgun may be offered for sale on one of the club's scratched ebony tables. I=Spaik am not fussy in this respect. After a suitable bout of haggling designed to massage the buyer's and seller's self-esteem, I would pay an exorbitant price without demur.

The city is simultaneously cheap and expensive. At the end of the ride my *vuspi* driver will demand ten times the fare an indigenous customer would have to pay. I=Spaik will give him half what he asks and, nodding acquiescently, listen to his conventional outpouring of abuse, complaints, and thanks. Only tourists pay any attention to the Naked Truth Club's price list for drinks. Like a few other foreigners, I=Spaik have attained the status of a privileged, tolerated outsider by assiduously patronizing the establishment and arbitrarily varying my tips: what I deposit on the table is roughly half the sum a genuine local would consider appropriate. I=Spaik can afford it. The Bureau has kept me punctually supplied with money – to the benefit of both parties. But for the regular materialization of my salary, I=Spaik would sooner or later have come to doubt the existence of my far-off employers and starved them of reports for good.

At the beginning of each month a taxi conveys me to the city's easternmost outskirts. There, surrounded by run-down housing developments, stands the largest of the four municipal bus stations. The huge block of left-luggage lockers is embedded in the rear wall of the main building. My taxi driver waits, engine idling, while I=Spaik run up the three steps to the little steel doors and, rubbing shoulders with some *chugg*-chewing peasant from the mountains, open my locker. The eastern bus station is the *chugg* trade's principal port of entry. The *chugg* shrub is cultivated in steep, terraced plantations on the south-facing slopes of the Eastern Range and harvested all year round. The smallholders and their families pick the leaf buds, store them in a dark, damp environment that fosters the growth of a silvery white, phosphorescent mould, and leave them to ferment. Good *chugg* is crumbly, has a mush-roomy flavour, and almost completely dissolves when chewed. When I=Spaik stand in front of the lockers, rising on tiptoe so as to reach the back of the compartment, the innumerable little pellets of fibre spat out and trodden flat by *chugg*-chewers form a springy, feltlike layer beneath my feet. The residue of this masticatory treat is the subject of a local proverb: '*Chugg* is the carpet of the poor.' Its purpose is to console them whenever they need help in some matter, whether great or small.

I have never met a foreigner whose constitution could tolerate *chugg* with ease. Any outsider prevailed upon to knead a handful of the mouldy leaf buds into a ball and pop it into his mouth is delighted at first by its mildly stimulating effect. According to Zinally, *chugg* is mainly an antidote to depression. Not for nothing is it the traditional drug of the old, who employ it as a palliative for the agonies of gout, the toothache occasioned by their last, rotting, suppurating molars, and the dawning realization that death is inevitable. In my early days here, I myself bought a bag of *chugg* from an old man's locker. While he looked on, chewing away, I tore open the grey envelope containing my salary and plucked a couple of banknotes from the thick, untidy wad of local and foreign currency. With a persistence I seldom display today, but for which I was once particularly noted in the service, I=Spaik made at least a dozen attempts to habituate myself to the drug. But like all Westerners – and, strangely enough, the Japanese – I lack a certain intestinal enzyme that enables the system to break it down. Within a few hours, I had to atone for my *chugg*-induced euphoria by suffering from watery diarrhoea and terrible stomach cramps.

The traffic is at a standstill. My *vuspi* driver vainly tries to sneak past on the outside, almost shaving the oncoming cars. An accident is blocking all three lanes of our carriageway. We manage to get through on the extreme right, but there the pavement is clogged with spectators. The motor scooter bores its way through them for some distance, but then we get stuck. The driver has trouble keeping his *vuspi* upright, and I=Spaik keep a precautionary right hand on the pocket that contains my ready cash. The key to my bus station locker was given me by my first and only contact man. Even now, in the enforced idleness of a traffic jam, I=Spaik can remember neither his name nor his face. The man in question, whose job it was to assist me during those early weeks, was the sports attaché of the Goethe Institute, which still existed at the time. Instead of remembering his name, I suddenly recall the first few digits of his long telephone number. Like members of trade missions and big foreign firms, he could be reached via the Luxor mobile phone system, which was still reliable in those days. The sports attaché must be dead, I'm sure. On the night of the third National Holiday, when the Gahists took advantage of the Cup Final to stage their unprecedented mass suicide – unprecedented, at least, in the city's recent history – panic broke out in the overcrowded football stadium. The bodies of those who had been suffocated or trampled to death lay on the pitch for days to come, awaiting identification by their next of kin, and local television ended each news broadcast by dwelling with malign persistence on the bluish faces of the foreign dead who had still to be retrieved. While recalling those silent close-ups, I am, after all, visited by a mental image of my erstwhile contact's face. The sports attaché was a chubby-cheeked, boyish-looking man. As seen on television, his eyes were wide with disbelief and the tip of his tongue protruded from between his clenched teeth. His collar, which was ripped to shreds, no longer concealed the gold chain whose little pendant crucifix had fitted perfectly into the hollow beneath his Adam's apple.

The traffic in the boulevard has sorted itself out. The vehicles on our side have taken possession of the innermost of the three opposite lanes and are using it up to the next lights. My *vuspi* passes the scene of the accident, a bumper-to-bumper collision involving half a dozen cars. The drivers are crouching in the shelter of their battered wrecks, discussing who should pay for what. As soon as the matter has been resolved, they will doubtless fetch an elder from the nearest side street, who will then, in return for a suitable fee, ensure that the oral agreements are kept. The People's Militia ignores the traffic except during parades and state visits, and these occasions have become infrequent. The National Holiday is no longer celebrated in style since the massacre in the stadium, and, discounting visits by the relevant UN commissioner in times of crisis, no senior foreign politician has shown his face in the city for several years.

I=Spaik saw no sign of blood or injury at the scene of the accident. If there were any casualties, they must already have been removed. Accident victims are a coveted form of merchandise, a kind of semi-finished product disputed by various middlemen. Hospital ambulances and the traditional rescue services have encountered successful competition from the motor-scooter ambulances developed by the ingenious Zeushene proprietor of a taxicab company. The injured are strapped to a narrow trailer, and a call centre peddles them to the hospital that bids most for them. They then become the hospital's property, body and soul, and their relations must sooner or later defray the cost of their treatment by paying a sum proportionate to the family's assets. Rumour has it that patients who cannot find anyone willing to make such a payment are compelled to purchase their release by donating a kidney or some bone marrow.

My *vuspi* driver takes advantage of the slowly unravelling traffic to engage in some daredevil changes of lane. My hands grip his belt buckle, my chin buries itself in his shoulder. Here, at the southern end of the boulevard, the road surface is particularly bad. The thin coat of tar on the old substratum is breaking up all over the place, and the exposed granite cobbles and slabs of sandstone are treacherously smooth, even in dry weather. If we crashed I'd be bound to break something, in which case the ambulance would probably take me to the former military hospital not far from here, on the eastern edge of the Goto. Its reputation is no worse than that of the city's other hospitals. Foreign nightclubbers who collapse after experimenting with new drugs or overindulging in old ones are often conveyed to its casualty department by helpful citizens eager to cash in. If I=Spaik recovered consciousness in one of its corridors, I would send word to Lieschen. Enlisted as a courier, a *vuspi* driver would race off to the rag-boilers' quarter and ferry her to the hospital. The clatter of her orthopaedic boots would herald my redemption: in her hand would be a plastic bag containing a thick wad of banknotes, the emergency reserve which I=Spaik keep in the deep-freeze compartment of the refrigerator on Lieschen's advice, concealed behind some frozen fish. This would be enough to purchase me the finest imported drugs, sterile dressings, and speedy conveyance to some bolthole of Lieschen's choosing.

But we don't crash: the club is already in sight. My driver steers his *vuspi* on to the broad pavement, swerves round the other two-wheelers parked there, and brakes to a halt. The youngsters from nouveau riche families who make up the bulk of the club's membership favour light motorcycles, off-road machines with high, stiltlike front forks, and Japanese motor scooters of certain makes. Knots of them are standing outside the entrance. There has for some time been a vogue for little yellow sunglasses which are never removed, even at night or in the club's dim interior. Another very popular accessory is the short, brightly coloured, ornamental quirt whose ancestor was the traditional donkey whip. The quirt-carrier uses it to slap his calf in time to his speech rhythms or exchange salutatory taps on the thigh or hip. I'm completely ignored – denied even such minor signs of contempt as an abrupt turn of the head or a cigarette butt tossed at my feet. The privileged youngsters' disdain for foreign residents is subject to fluctuations: derisive interest alternates with phases of total disregard.

Above the entrance is a pale blue neon sign: just the word 'Club' written in an elongated script of pseudo-oriental appearance. I=Spaik had always assumed that the Naked Truth Club's name was a kind of joke until Doc Zinally explained that it refers to some saying of the Great Gahis. Consequently, foreign patrons of the club are strongly advised not to mention the name in a sarcastic or humorous context, and the wisest policy, undoubtedly, is never to let it escape one's lips.

15 Arrogance

Although the only word that glowed above the entrance, picked out in soft blue neon lettering, was 'Club', we needed no confirmation that we had reached the establishment we sought. Assembled outside the Naked Truth Club were youngsters whose parents' money left them free to concentrate on higher things, on designer drugs, on art and truths of every kind. Their families' wealth, so Zinally had told us, was seldom older and often even younger than its callow beneficiaries. Nouveau riche families put their affluence on display. It varied with fluctuations in the inflation rate and was regenerated by the surges in securities and foreign exchange rates that pulsed through the city's white and black economies.

This morning, when we slid our old-fashioned travellers' cheques across the hotel reception desk, we were handed two thick wads of banknotes in exchange. Three categories of the *lewi*, the city's principal form of currency, are in circulation: old, recent, and new. These three generations have a relative value of one to ten to a hundred. The highest-denomination banknote remains the new ten-thousand *lewi*, which has gold thread woven into it, but the main, everyday medium of payment is the newly issued, orange five-hundred, the first banknote to bear Gahis's portrait. Freddy told us that this almost photographic likeness of the Prophet of the Revolution has been the National Bank's smartest move to date in its endeavour to stabilize the national currency. Gahis's reputation was growing day by day, he said. It would never occur to anyone to scrawl a telephone number on the new five-hundred or roll it up for use as an earwax extractor, as people so often did with other banknotes.

The city's moneyed *jeunesse* greeted our arrival with covert curiosity. There was even a hint of friendly approval in the eyes that watched us as we entered the club. Although products of pure chance and whim, our haircuts were certainly a point in our favour because they almost exactly matched the youngsters' prevailing style. You were particularly entranced by their little yellow sunglasses, which had struck us as singularly pointless outside, in the brightness of the urban night, but which many of them wore in the club's gloomy interior. We took a booth near the stage, which was empty but already bathed in a green spotlight. Astonished by the bar prices, which were far higher than those at the Esperanza, we ordered a *zuleika* apiece and some of the big, three-year fruit of the fatnut tree. The music was loud – sustained notes slurred by a singer with a very high-pitched voice. The words of the song were in Piddi-Piddi, but rendered almost unintelligible to our unpractised ears by the flirtatiously pseudo-archaic way in which he sang them. After we had listened to the loudspeaker above our heads for a while, you suddenly became convinced that it was a love song, a lament inspired by unrequited passion.

Kuhl had regretted while briefing us in Cyprus that it was impossible, in the short time available, to show us one of Spaik's reports in full. Soon after his unauthorized departure from the Esperanza, Spaik had begun to commit flagrant breaches of the rules governing reports from overseas agents. His messages to the Bureau via American World Net soon comprised twice, then three times the permissible number of letters. Spaik's legendary dagger-thrust report dating from his first year in place, a sheaf of sixty sheets when printed out, began by confining itself to the pest-control techniques practised in the city. It was only when he got to the passage dealing with the campaign against the European Croton bug, which had found itself a new dispersion area far from home, that minor mix-ups and bizarre spelling mistakes indicated that he was approaching the real nub of his report. Some curiously esoteric rather than medical reflections on the transmission of hepatitis by household parasites were abruptly followed by a crystal-clear account of the assassination that had yet to take place. Three days after Spaik's report came in, an American four-star general was murdered during an off-the-record visit to an air base in south-east Turkey. An elderly Turkish Air Force colonel stationed there, who had once been trained as a radar expert in the United States, drove a dagger into the distinguished visitor's liver and then took his own life. Uttering Gahis's famous last words, which were even translated into German after news of the murder broke, he fell on the bloody weapon with such force and accuracy that he contrived to transfix his heart.

Although Kuhl probably knew we were acquainted with this story, it being one of the Bureau's favourite anecdotes, he refrained from making play with any subsequent and equally spectacular feats of intelligence-gathering on his protégé's part. It is said that this first great prediction of Spaik's embodied one of those anomalies typical of his later reports: the name of the Turkish assassin was correctly spelt and reproduced in full, whereas his victim, the skewered general, was referred to only by his two incorrectly spelt forenames, the second of which was entirely unknown to the public because the ambitious soldier had dropped it at the start of his career. This forename, spurned by its bearer but revived in modified form by Spaik, we encountered as a surname in the Naked Truth Club, because the waitress who brought our order and sat down beside you, uninvited, introduced herself as Leila Calvin.

Miss Calvin opened the conversation in halting American English but, when we replied in Piddi-Piddi, promptly switched to the urban lingua franca, which tripped off her tongue with twittering fluency, and gratefully commended our linguistic skill. She was extremely fidgety. Even her walk had struck us as exaggeratedly bouncy, as if she were kept earthbound by insufficient gravity. Now, as she sat there with her fingertips resting on the edge of the table like aids to balance, she seemed to be floating on a wafer-thin cushion of air that imparted pneumatic thrusts to her pelvis at irregular intervals, spasms that communicated themselves to her torso, making it twitch convulsively, and usually culminated in a jerk of the left shoulder or a tilt of the chin. Miss Calvin did not ask where we hailed from or what had brought us to the city. Evidently, our mere presence in the Naked Truth Club lent us enough of a background in itself. She asked us to call her by her first name and listed what the club had for sale: not only souvenirs but a variety of personal services that could, without more ado, be administered in darkened booths while the stage show was in progress. Patrons fond of their creature comforts could rent upstairs rooms by the quarter-hour. Also available for the enjoyment of one form of service or another were the cubicles in the men's room, which were scrupulously clean and could be securely locked.

Leila Calvin permitted us to stand her a Cuba Libre. Sucking it up through a chocolate-coated straw, she informed us, at our request, of the personal services she herself could offer patrons of the club. With a touch of pride, the Naked Truth Club's waitress described herself as an aphorist: she perpetuated one of her native city's honourable traditions by composing maxims and mottoes. Like the ancients, she subscribed to the rule that no truly effective epigram could comprise more than nine words. Moreover, every saying she coined was unique, being inscribed only once, and in a calligraphic style, on a small hempen card. The box from which the purchaser could extract his epigram never held fewer than three hundred and thirty-three of these cards, so the uniqueness of the pearl of wisdom he acquired was guaranteed. Miss Calvin told us that she had, as usual, left her fortune-telling box

with the barman, and that one of us would be entitled to
draw a card at once in return for three of the new five-
hundreds. Naturally, we accepted her offer without a
moment's hesitation. She hurried over to the bar, but the
acquisition of our oracular pronouncement was temporarily delayed by the start of the stage show.

The club was now quite crowded, and when the music
stopped and nearly all the lights went out the gloom was
filled with a strangely sibilant murmur. It sounded as if the
members of the audience had already endured too long a
wait and were now determined, in their collective annoyance, to make the first performer atone for it. And indeed,
no sooner had he mounted the stage than he was assailed
by a chorus of whistles and piercing cries, and it seemed to
us that the figure in the green spotlight was being greeted
not only by terms of abuse but by defamatory phrases
specially coined for the occasion. Portly and bearded but
very young, he stood on the edge of the stage with a cord-
less microphone in his hands. He wore a costume con-
sisting of a kind of red plastic caftan and a huge, voluminous turban, and whenever he moved his head the
latter swung to and fro with a metronomic regularity that
suggested it contained a propulsive device of some kind.
The poet launched into his recitation without any preamble,
and at once a reverent hush descended. He spoke into the
microphone in a high-pitched squawk, clicking his tongue
and smacking his lips. We soon gathered that he was
reeling off the designations of internationally well-known
firms, but he subjected their syllabic sequences to unusual
stresses and rhythms that distorted the conventional sound

patterns of these venerable brand names. We were amazed at how many of them the poet submitted to this treatment. It was as if he were robbing his audience's memory of every firm and product they had ever heard of. We recognized the trisyllabic name of a long-defunct German electrical engineering concern whose tonal possibilities he explored at least a dozen times in a goatlike bleat. He then fired off, with heroic bravura, a series of automobile marques that had gone down in the annals of technology. Having blossomed once more, the metaphorical splendour of these names faded away into a long murmur, into ever bolder distortions of the word 'Volkswagen'. Our first impression of the city's creativity, this interminable poem, simple in conception but vast in extent, appealed to us more and more. We ordered another *zuleika*, and you hazarded the possibility that this voluble poet might long ago, without our noticing, have also recited the names of future firms still gestating in the uterus of worldwide entrepreneurism.

This conjecture became a certainty when the poet, having at first swung his turban and caftan only, proceeded to amplify his recital with gestures and physical contortions. All that he conjured up with pointed fingers, twisted limbs, and little dance steps was unmistakably sexual in connotation, and it was a pleasure to see and hear him convey how intercourse was taking place between the firms he cited, whether existing, defunct, or awaiting parturition. Dr Zinally had told us that the Naked Truth Club's name was based on a passage from the Great Gahis's last televised address. In this speech, delivered just before his death, the Prophet of the Revolution had made his first pronouncement on the nature of human truth, comparing it – to the surprise of many of his adherents – to a bitch in heat. In a unique series of verses, Gahis had apparently poured scorn on any attempt to disguise the fecundity of a truth in heat, and Zinally deplored the fact that no videotape of this, the Master's last televised appearance, had been allowed to reach the open market.

16 Congeniality

My favourite place in the club is a secluded nook on the left, the banquette beside the door to the men's room. Sitting there, I=Spaik am fortunately spared the sight of Baba Bey rocking his outsize turban on-stage. This is the third time in the past few days that my poor ears have been subjected to his commercial copulation number, and I find its conception and performance as incomprehensible as ever. Baba Bey is approaching his finale. It's all about the decline of the American telephone companies, the disintegration of their regional monopolies, and the rise of the new international telecommunications giants. If I have correctly interpreted Baba Bey's dance, his words, and the interjections of his audience, his allegory for this economic process is a kind of round dance in which big public companies present their bare bottoms to the ones behind, are duly mounted, and simultaneously sodomize the ones in front.

Little Calvin still hasn't found time to serve me. He knows my sluggish bulk won't run away, and the two young foreigners who entered the club shortly after me impress him as more promising customers. Calvin puts his oracle box on the table in front of the pair. Only one of them reaches inside, but they put their heads together over the card he pulls out as if the inscription on it guarantees them a common destiny. Seated cheek by jowl like that, they remind me of the tourists who tried to coax me to join them at my former table at the Esperanza. They may even be the same ones. I can hear them laughing from my alcove. It seems they like the meaning of the nine words in Piddi-Piddi which Calvin has inscribed on the little red card in pseudo-oriental calligraphy. Now they're stroking his cheek. Fidgety as ever, the little creature is rocking to and fro. He's wearing the violet pleated miniskirt that would cover his frilly panties only if he kept still. It's not long since this revealing outfit earned him a visit to the men's room, where he was thrashed with beaded ornamental whips until he bled. One blow narrowly missed his left eye, and the eyebrow needed stitches. Calvin told me he had to promise to oblige the cosmetic surgeon, a Syrian expatriate, for an indefinite period before the latter would agree to continue to treat the scar professionally.

Calvin takes his oracle box back to the bar, nodding to me as he walks past. The box is his second and, in the long term, his only asset, because he's beginning to age perceptibly, at least in the harsh neon glare of the men's room, although he may pass for a girl a while longer in the dim lighting upstairs. Foreigners who visit the Naked Truth Club are avid for Calvin's epigrams. There are nights when I=Spaik have seen him sell a good dozen of his cards. Westerners eager to know their fate quite often ask him for another card the same night, as if the wisdom already imparted will be rendered more potent by a second helping. On such occasions Calvin skilfully hedges and prevaricates till dawn, citing the position of the moon and other higher powers. Then, just before the bar closes, he pronounces the moment auspicious after all, and, with an alluring swirl of his miniskirt, once more carries the oracle box over to the table, which is now awash with *zuleika*.

Freddy predicts that Calvin will come to a bad end. He says he'll be found tied up and dumped face down in one of the Goto's reeking sewers – hitherto the fate of every local inhabitant rash enough to bastardize the Great Gahis's work. I=Spaik don't know whether Calvin's aphorisms are really, as Freddy claims, clumsy digests of Gahis's ideas. My fingers have never plucked a card from the oracle box, nor do I know Gahis's canticles and sermons except at second hand. At one time or another we foreign residents have all acquired the nine-cassette version subtitled in Piddi-Piddi, which can be purchased for a tourist price at any of the larger stalls in the video bazaars. But the tapes lie there unseen. We don't even tear off their transparent protective wrappers. Something about the plain white covers, which bear nothing but Gahis's name and the numerals 1 to 9, seems to deter us. We eventually put the video cassettes away and lose sight of them. To discover the whereabouts of my copies of the Prophet's canticles, I= Spaik would have to consult Lieschen.

Calvin is carrying a tray laden with five or six bottles of Crimean champagne. The red, semi-dry variety has become fashionable in recent months. A youngster will take big swigs straight from the bottle and, on putting it down, pull a strange face as if surprised at his own predilection. Empty bottles are hurled at the stage with increasing frequency

Georg Klein

these days, but to the best of my knowledge no poet has yet
been seriously injured.

Baba Bey has relinquished the green spotlight to a novice,
a young Zeushene. The latter is wearing the traditional
catskin bonnet but has tied it on his head with a broad pink
silk ribbon in such a way that the bow at his throat
resembles an airplane propeller. The debutant starts to sing,
accompanying himself on a tiny keyboard which he rests
on his hip and plays with one forefinger in a touchingly
amateurish manner. He begins with the form of words that
traditionally introduces Zeushene pastoral songs: 'When
milk was still grass, and grass was still earth, and earth was
still rock . . .' Despite my swollen bladder, this courageous
opening prompts me to pause in the doorway that leads to
the men's room. But the handsome youth does not, unfortunately, get much further. Something about him must have
aroused the audience's immediate displeasure, because the
first salvo of bottles hits the boards with a concerted thud.
In my compassionate reluctance to witness his ignominious
departure from the stage, I=Spaik quickly set off down the
sloping passage that leads to the men's room.

It was down here in the harsh lighting of the anteroom
that I first set eyes on little Calvin. Not yet permitted to
serve in the club, he had to sit behind a small table among
the washbasins. He sold perfumes, wet wipes, tiny tubes of
Vaseline, and the silver hairslides with which men used at
one time to keep the long hair on their temples from flop-
ping over their ears. That fashion went out ages ago. Calvin
himself, who used to have a ponytail, now sports a military
crew-cut with his miniskirts and silk blouses. In my whim-

sical way, however, I like to remember how he used to look, perhaps because I found his seated figure a sight for sore eyes. Although condemned to sit on the stool behind his little table, his bottom was always in motion. Something made him fidget all the time. His shoulders slid up and down the black wall tiles, and attending to a well-heeled foreign customer like me made him more fidgety still. While my eyes roamed over his wares he abandoned a sitting position altogether. With the undersides of his thighs barely touching the wooden stool and his knees slightly bent, he stood facing me in the bright red, elasticated needlecord slacks he always wore. Even now that Calvin wears pleated miniskirts and Freddy's houseboys appeal to me more, the iridescence of recollection makes me realize why the Spaik of those days could not resist taking red-trousered Calvin into one of the securely lockable lavatory cubicles with a view to enjoying some small favour or other.

No one inherited Calvin's table when he was promoted to become a waiter, but the club's video vendor, a distant relation of his, has included the most important of his wares in the assortment on his tray. Calvin got him the job when the first video clips of the club poets came on the market. Ever since then, the toothless, *chugg*-chewing old codger has spent his nights in the doorway between the washroom and the urinals with the tray suspended from his neck by broad leather straps. He's standing there now, and he sees me coming. He'll make a sale or two during the inter-mission after the third number, when members of the audience come streaming downstairs. The old man's wood-en tray bars my path, but he declines to take half a step backwards for me. I squeeze past, and just as I draw level with him he spits a big ball of *chugg* fibre over my shoulder into the nearest urinal.

Such incidents are a routine part of my life in the city, so it must be my expectation of a successor that alters my view of them. While emptying my bladder, I develop a vision of the response the elderly expectorator merits. On the way back I pause in front of him and insinuate my hands beneath his wooden tray. I'm surprised at my own strength. I've done nothing in recent years to keep my muscles strong and supple. There's a sound like teeth snapping, but it's probably only the hard plastic cases of some audiotapes splintering on the old man's forehead and cheekbones. He topples over backwards and lies there with the wooden tray concealing his face. My heart pounds madly, my right hand hurts, and I enjoy every aspect of what I can see.

Among the scattered merchandise I discern a single square of shiny black cardboard. I know, even before I stoop to pick it up, that it must enclose a Black CD. The Black CD is not for sale on the open market, and any foreigner attempting to acquire one runs risks of an imponderable nature. It carries the whole of the Great Gahis's last television broadcast, which lasted over an hour, and is the soundtrack of the video recording of which no copy has ever, so far as I know, been released for sale. Doc Zinally told me that Freddy owns a Black CD, and that one night after a steam bath, being a regular customer, he was invited to Freddy's private quarters to listen to it. His host seemed to need an accomplice, because Zinally soon became convinced that Freddy, too, was listening to Gahis's final speech for the first time. They sat on a small couch cheek to cheek, sharing the earphones of a headset at full stretch. The Prophet's last televised address did not differ in essence from his nine videotaped canticles. As usual, the Great Gahis employed a loose synthesis of all the dialects and idioms commonly used in the city. He, Zinally, would only have understood the passages in Piddi-Piddi if Freddy hadn't simultaneously interpreted many of the others in a whisper. The Prophet's address to his followers in the heyday of liberation, at the zenith of Gahist power, amounted to a reprimand. After making some dark predictions relating to the immediate future, his speech culminated in that mysterious, chanted passage about the bitchlike nature of truth. Only a few verses long, this broke off abruptly, and all that followed the ultimate labial was the sound of rending silk and a dull thud.

Being the person I am, I stoop and retrieve the Black CD from the lavatory's tiles. A rivulet of bright red blood is trickling from under the vendor's tray, following the camber of the floor and flowing toward the gutter beneath the urinals. I thrust the CD into my open-necked shirt. It slithers over my left nipple and comes to rest on my protuberant belly. The Great Gahis is said to have pierced his white robe with the point of a traditional curved dagger. The video reputedly shows how a powerful gush of blood turned the thin, silken material red in an instant. The Prophet's final, right-handed jerk of the weapon's handle was obviously intended to enlarge the wound and rupture the intestines the dagger-point had transfixed. Then the camera pans up to give a brief glimpse of the studio's overhead gantry before a spot directed at the lens causes a black-bordered, flickering flare. A final noise, recorded and broadcast before the transmission broke off, must be assumed to be the sound of Gahis's body hitting the floor or, more likely, his head striking the edge of the table.

17 Pleasure

Leila Calvin watched us wide-eyed as we spurned the silver nutcrackers and tackled the shells of the three-year fatnuts with thumb and forefinger alone. The secret, it soon transpired, was to exert just enough pressure to enable the soft kernels to emerge intact from their shattered shells. We're aware of our manual strength and sensitive touch. Years of training have instilled a love of the one-to-one exercises in which, locking hands with each other, we develop the tensile strength of our fingers, and we've always derived especial pleasure, when undertaking a mission for the Enforcement Branch, from operating on a subject four-handed. The kernel of the fatnut resembles that of a walnut in shape and texture, but is unappealingly grey and covered with a tough, transparent skin. Leila Calvin quoted a saying of Gahis's that enlisted an old local proverb for application to the Gahist movement: 'The fatnut's unsightly appearance vouches for its extra sweetness.' We held half a particularly convoluted-looking fatnut to her lips, and she took the morsel between her bared teeth to avoid smudging her orange lipstick.

Although the club had filled up, more and more people seemed to be crowding in. From time to time, one of those who squeezed past our table would bend down and offer his services in Piddi-Piddi, American English, poor French, or even – on one occasion – passable German. They were all sufficiently impressed by Leila Calvin's curt, snarling ripostes to let themselves be borne away on the human tide, muttering and cursing as they went. We couldn't understand what Miss Calvin said that fended off their advances, but we gathered that she regarded us as her personal quarry, and the thought did not displease us.

After a brief intermission, the show resumed with a double act. Two brothers – one-eyed twins, no less – mounted the stage, each carrying a tall chair resembling a bar stool. Having sat down facing each other and exchanged a long, searching stare, as if trying to detect some unusual physiognomical feature, they proceeded to sing at each other in a bellow. We asked Leila Calvin what language they were using, but she said it was just a form of mouth music. Many of the newer poets would study it with positively archaeological zeal, she said, trying to unearth traditional usages, extinct lyrics, and forgotten narrative techniques. Her cousin, who worked at the institute for the study and preservation of the oral traditions of desert and steppe tribes, could tell a host of amusing stories about the newer poets' aspirations. Apparently, they spent whole afternoons in the institute's sound archive, listening with headsets over their hot ears to recordings made decades ago by foreign ethnologists. The young fellows could be heard humming with their eyes shut, singing along at the tops of their voices, or stamping their feet. Her cousin and the institute's second technician, a cousin of her mother's, often played the tapes at twice the correct speed to encourage the poets to join in with even more of a will, performing regular lap dances and singing with laryngeal fervour.

Leila Calvin knew where the brothers, whose singing we quite enjoyed, had got the inspiration for their duet. The words they hurled from stool to stool were taken from the male-voice chants of the Egichaeans, an extinct minority once resident in the city. The twins had succeeded, via American World Net, in recording a religious service held by an immigrant community in Toronto. Egichaeism's very ancient ecclesiastical language, a crude mixture of ancient Greek and Aramaic interlarded with snippets of Latin, Arabic, and even Old Persian, was wholly unintelligible to the young poets and had for that very reason, because of its acoustic beauty alone, inspired them to create mouth music and neologisms of their own. Leila Calvin claimed to know the singers well. Like them, she had attended the American Baptist Mission's language course in the days before that institution, together with almost every other foreign educational establishment, had been closed down for security reasons. The twins were very interested in conversing with educated foreign visitors, she said, and would certainly be willing to join us at our table after their performance.

We declined Leila's offer with thanks, so she promptly made another suggestion. She felt sure we'd heard of *chugg*, the miraculous shrub of *Arabian Nights* fame. In one of the rooms upstairs one could chew the finest *chugg* and wash it down with vintage *zuleika* brandy. Really old *zuleika* brandy was almost unobtainable on the open market – one had to have contacts among the families who distilled the rare spirit in the former Egichaean quarter. Even foreigners who had been resident in the city for years seldom managed to develop such connections, said Leila, so visitors were doubly disadvantaged. Only the simultaneous consumption of vintage *zuleika* brandy made it possible for Europeans, Americans, and Japanese – the latter were particularly vulnerable – to partake of *chugg* without suffering any unpleasant after-effects. *Zuleika* brandy alone contained sufficient quantities of an enzyme that enabled their sensitive intestines to tolerate the drug. Dr Lynch Zinally had warned us against *chugg* and drawn our attention to the fact that foreigners were often encouraged, with the aid of lies and subterfuges of all kinds, to partake of *chugg* and alcohol at the same time. The adventurous tourist usually recovered consciousness in some backyard or other, robbed and sullied with vomit and excrement. As if that were not humiliating enough, he also had to suffer a local doctor to thrust a tube down his gullet and pump out his stomach.

We smilingly accepted Leila Calvin's invitation and vacated our table for the use of other patrons of the Naked Truth Club. The pleated miniskirt tittuped on ahead of us. It was only in the crush that our guide's diminutive stature became really apparent. High heels notwithstanding, she barely came up to most men's shoulders. And suddenly – as if physical size and gender were logically interrelated – we started looking around for some female patrons. Zinally had told us that the local tribes' genetic vitality was strikingly demonstrated by the tall stature of their girls and women. We hadn't noticed a single female in the club, nor, however much we stood on tiptoe and craned our necks, could we see one anywhere. Having momentarily lost sight of Leila Calvin, we rediscovered her in an alcove beside the door to the lavatories. She fumbled under her skirt, then thrust a package of some kind across the table into the outspread fingers of a man. Her customer, slumped in the furthest corner of his banquette, was sitting in a poor light. As we passed him, however, we thought we recognized him as the down-at-heel Italian who had encountered us on the terrace of the Esperanza.

We followed Leila Calvin upstairs into a passage lined with numerous doors, one of which she unlocked for us to reveal a small room containing nothing but a bed, a chair, and a small cupboard, which could be opened with the door key. This held an array of glasses and a few smallish copper vessels. From behind a hookah of handsome workmanship Leila Calvin produced a small leather pouch. While she was eagerly but maladroitly fumbling with the drawstring, we seized the opportunity to sandwich her between us. You knocked the pouch of *chugg* out of her hand and whispered to her that we knew perfectly well how locals contrived to rob foreigners. Our fingers insinuated themselves into her sweaty armpits from behind. She was such a lightweight that we needed only one hand apiece to hoist her into the air between us. We let her dangle awhile, feet kicking. One shoe came off, then the other. Her orange-daubed mouth gasped for breath, disclosing her small and rather carious teeth. Silently, we held Leila Calvin aloft, then laid our free hands on her shapely throat, kneaded her surprisingly masculine Adam's apple, and let our fingers roam from her swollen carotids to the clean-shaven nape of her neck. Then we went to work with both hands at once. We stretched her cervical vertebrae, applying carefully gauged pressure to her jaw and cheek-bones, and threatened to remove the hands that were holding her up by her armpits. The short drop, or, to be more precise, the accelerative force exerted on her neck, would be enough to dislocate one or two cervical vertebrae – and that, given a little bad luck, could have dire conse-quences. She went quite still and, barely moving her lips, asked in a whisper what we wanted of her. You put your mouth to her ear, took it between your teeth, and gently nibbled its cartilaginous convolutions. Her earring tinkled softly against your dental enamel. At length you told her whom we were looking for. We boldly claimed to know that she was acquainted with Spaik. To our delight, she not only conceded this at once but informed us, in the next breath, that he was sitting downstairs in the club. He was, she said, the man at whose alcove she had briefly paused before we came upstairs together.

It may have been remiss of us to have given Leila Calvin only a punch or two in the stomach and kidneys. Scrawny little bodies are quite often tougher than one imagines, and the pain in the gut that so thoroughly demoralizes bulky subjects can actually lead, in the case of lightweights, to the strangest surges of strength – even to the euphoric courage born of despair. We probably allowed ourselves to be seduced by the beauty of the moment: Leila was writhing, doubled up, on the little room's shabby oriental carpet with her hands clutching her stomach and her twitching heels drawn up to her frilly panties.

18 Magnanimity

The concealed door opens and Calvin bursts forth. At first it looks as if he means to hurry past my table, but he abruptly turns and flops down in my alcove. The hatchway situated between my regular place and the ramp that leads to the lavatories is papered over and has no handle, so it's easy to miss. It gives access to an iron spiral staircase, the shortest route to the two floors above, and is used by members of the staff when speed is essential. Being a patron of long standing, I'm sufficiently conversant with the club's customs to have a pretty fair idea of who and what are conveyed up and down the stairs by this route, though I myself have never had to raise the flap, which silently hinges upwards, and squeeze through the narrow gap. Calvin's face is smeared with snot and lipstick, and tears have made his mascara run. I grip his shoulder, intending to ask what has happened to him in the few minutes since we clinched our little deal, but he frees himself with a jerk. He stares at me, breathing heavily, then spits in my face, grabs me by the hair, and drags me out of the alcove. With surprising strength, he tows me over to the hatchway that has just ejected him in such a seemingly wretched state.

No sooner has the sprung flap come to rest behind us

than he collapses at the foot of the staircase, writhing and gasping as if the mere act of lying there causes him pain. He also curses me, but it obviously hurts him to blurt out these imprecations, and I'm soon hard put to it to make out a single word, he's stammering and whimpering so much. I haul him to his feet and give him a little shake. Speaking more distinctly now, he tells me – if I correctly interpret his remarks, which flit from one urban dialect to another – that I must make good my escape by way of the backyard: my smiling compatriots, he says, are after my stinking hide. I release him, whereupon he sinks to his knees and starts crawling up the spiral staircase on all fours. That's how I come to see that his hitched-up miniskirt is wet, and that his frilly panties are clinging, damply and transparently, to his buttocks. Calvin senses my gaze and smooths the skirt down as far as its brevity permits. Then he turns once more to face me and, in clearest Piddi-Piddi, quotes a famous saying of the Great Gahis: 'Young rats sniff out the spot where the old rat swam across the river the year before.' I have never fathomed why the Gahists find this dictum so meaningful, and I find it all the harder to understand how it can now be applied, in its most literal sense, to me and the man sent to succeed me. For one long, blissfully surprising moment, I once more see the Bureau as it was in the springtime of my posting here: a treasure trove of knowledge and a hand that knew when to give and when to take. I thank Calvin, who has meanwhile crawled some way up the staircase, extract as many five-hundreds as I can find from my wad of banknotes, and pass them up to him. It so happens that there are exactly the same number as I paid for what he procured for me. He stows them under his skirt and points out the door to the backyard.

It is only an unwritten law that foreigners may not enter the Goto. No checkpoints threaten pedestrians or vehicles in any of the narrow streets leading to the oldest part of the city. Taxi drivers quite often make a detour through the Goto's streets when there's a traffic jam in Freedom of Speech Boulevard. They then ask their foreign passengers to draw the curtains over the rear window and confine themselves to peeping through the crack. The impression one gleans of life in the streets is disappointing: nothing, at first glance, seems to differentiate it from the daily routine in other ancient quarters of the city. It is only when some child or old man draws back a skinny arm and hurls a stone at the taxi's bodywork that the foreigner peering through the crack in the curtains blenches at the realization that the locals regard him as a spy, a parasite preying on the secret of the Goto.

My two eyes, still equally sharp-sighted at the time, first saw the Goto from the river, which flows round the quarter in a semicircle and encloses the hills on which it stands. The current is sluggish, and the tide forces the river's brackish waters back up the marshy inlets as far as the city itself when the moon is full. At such times it gives off an acrid, putrid stench, and city children wielding nets and primitive rods catch the tasty brackish-water perch, which is usually brought to market only by the fishermen of outlying districts. When darkness falls, members of the Cyrenian minority attired in their traditional blue robes gather by the light of the full moon and walk in procession, singing, to their places of prayer on the river bank. Youngsters from other religious communities make fun of this and accompany them on their motorcycles. They circle the procession, revving their engines, tooting their horns, and yelling obscene questions which remain unanswered. There is an enduring but quite unsubstantiated belief in the city that the Cyrenians' nocturnal devotions at full moon are associated with sexual orgies.

If Freddy's fund of historical anecdotes is to be believed, the last massacre of the Cyrenians was perpetrated a thousand years ago, when a Mongol army, intent on looting the city, launched its one and only attack from downstream. Although the city's history abounds in pogroms and bloodbaths, the Cyrenian minority was not subjected to any outrages worth mentioning in the centuries that followed. From an outsider's standpoint, the Cyrenian ethnic group seems positively to invite spontaneous slaughter. It is small and weak and rendered unusually conspicuous by its peculiar customs. That the Cyrenians have been spared for a thousand years must be attributable to the humiliating trade they pursue. Cyrenian families earn a living mainly by disposing of sewage. They also act as the city's knackers and destroyers of vermin. Their mule carts drive through the rag-boilers' quarter, where I live, to empty the cesspits in the sewerless streets and deliver the bundles of chopped straw commonly employed to soak up the liquid content of the latrines.

I myself have twice availed myself of the services of a Cyrenian pest controller, once to rid the house of cockroaches immediately after I moved in, and again only lately, when our roof became one of the routes used by rats on their way to the food markets. Lieschen had heard the nightly patter of feet. Traps were set, and the cries of the dying animals carried to my quarters down below. The Cyrenian rat-catcher returned at least a dozen times to install lethal contrivances capable of outwitting the artful rodents in a variety of novel ways. In the end, one of his sons lay in wait on the roof for a week, night after night, to dispatch any lone animals straying across the neighbouring roofs with a silent, bolt-firing device resembling a crossbow.

Lieschen kept the hunter company every night. I know this because the adolescent boy asked me at dawn after his first vigil – timidly, because he expected to be punished – whether it was permissible for her to do so. By the time I hauled my *zuleika*-sodden carcass upstairs by the banisters a few days later, the boy had grown bolder: he asked if he might let Lieschen fire his weapon. He must have interpreted my stupefied gaze as an affirmative, because he promptly disappeared in the direction of the ladder to the roof space, and I've no doubt that he alone, and not Lieschen, had been waiting to see how I reacted to the news of her desire to shoot rats. She probably accompanied the boy and their joint haul to the Goto, where the rat-catchers cremate their dead rodents aboard the big grey lighters that line the river bank. Fires smoulder day and night on these flat monsters, which are more like pontoons than boats. This is where the Cyrenians make their celebrated soap – I'm told it can even be bought these days in the duty-free shops at German airports – out of animal fat, ash, mineral powder, and vegetable extracts. Even when very plump, however, rats are never used in soap manufacture. The Cyrenians regard them as animals formerly sacred but subsequently cast out by God. They merit a certain respect even when killed, and are therefore incinerated in separate fires with a small admixture of sweet-smelling wood.

I walk down to the river, which I haven't set eyes on for years. Calvin's package reposes, still unopened, in the breast pocket of my jacket. Its gratifyingly irksome pressure on my ribs can be felt at every step. I have an urge to make for the landing stage used by the pleasure boats that wait there for adventurous foreign tourists after dark. Simply but quite skilfully converted for the purpose, these former naval craft operate only at night to avoid courting trouble. When the moon is full, as it is tonight, its light alone is sufficient to convey an impression of the majestic blue-clay architecture on the hills of the Goto. The Great Gate of Prophecy, with its three bulky columns, faces the harbour barely two hundred yards from the water. As for the Blue Dome, a windowless rotunda and the largest monoportal building in the world, this can clearly be seen beyond some medieval warehouses as soon as the boat trains its spotlight on the cupola.

No sooner has the massive building been caressed by the spotlight's luminous finger than the first shots ring out. Pleasure boats regularly come under fire from the Goto bank of the river, but the former naval vessels' armour-plating and thick, safety-glass windows afford sufficient protection from small-arms fire. Only one really serious attack has ever been launched, according to Freddy, and that occurred during the turbulent days preceding the first anniversary of Gahis's death. On that occasion, one of the pleasure boats was hit by a genuine antitank rocket, an ancient NATO weapon of Franco-German manufacture. It exploded in the midst of a group of multimedia salesmen from Singapore, putting them out of business for good.

19 Piety

Spaik's seat in the tiny alcove was still warm when we ran our hands over the upholstery. We sniffed the back of the banquette and caught a whiff of the stench the squalid fellow had left behind. Lying on the table was a small brass tin containing two identical tablets and one large, duotone capsule. You pocketed this pillbox and we asked the barman where Spaik was. He said that Spaik had just left the club by the front entrance. Outside, a youth leaning against his motorcycle readily told us which way the malodorous old man had gone. We tried to catch him up – we even jogged some way along the boulevard, but the pavement was thronged with pedestrians. Besides, our haste attracted attention and caused annoyance. When a candy vendor, with unmistakably evil intent, pushed his handcart into your path and only your quick reactions saved you from falling headlong, we abandoned the chase. Pausing at a coffee stall, we resigned ourselves to the probability that Spaik had long since hailed a taxi or turned off down a side street. He had escaped us once more. There was still time to find him again, however, so we indulged ourselves: we sipped our hot coffee in leisurely fashion, and you liberally sweetened the strong brew with aromatic, coarse-grained brown sugar.

It was only when we started to cross the bridge, strolling along arm in arm, that we noticed the moon hovering above the river to our right, low in the sky and very big. The outlines of the orange disk were irregular, like a child's drawing. This was the huge orange moon for which the region is famous. Kuhl had mentioned that it flitted through Spaik's reports in an abstruse manner. Apparently, Spaik almost always touched on the moon and its shape and colour, which he described in florid, rambling, disastrously misspelt prose, before his report succinctly divulged its true message, the really hot news. We ourselves were not unmoved by this full moon. What amazed us most of all was the clarity of its silhouette, which seemed to display dents and protrusions – indeed, serrations and sharp notches – on the edge of the disk. It might have been excised from the hazy urban sky with a knife.

As we leant on the parapet side by side, our biceps nestling against each other, a strangely naval-looking pleasure boat emerged from under the bridge and glided slowly moonward. That was when we realized we had an unobstructed view of the forbidden quarter. The dark but glinting mass of buildings on the right bank could only be the Goto. Ever since Gahis's death, or for the past nine years, the quarter has been unlit at night. Radical believers among the many splinter groups into which the Gahists have disintegrated infer from allusions in the Prophet's last videotaped sermon that he advocated a strict ban on illuminating the environs of sacred places at night. Kuhl commented in detail on the conjecture that Spaik had gone to ground in the Goto. This suspicion was based, he said, on a data-processing analysis of his reports, which the Bureau always received via American World Net. It could be assumed with a relatively high degree of probability that Spaik transmitted them from the former Baptist Mission in the Goto. On the other hand, the city's telecommunications links were in such a chaotic state that they defied even partial elucidation. American World Net had in recent years become the leading regional provider of access to the Internet. Only a second-rater by international standards, this company owed its success to the special terms it offered institutions of a religious and ideological nature. Now that various Christian sects and foundations were majority stockholders in American World Net, the company's worldwide message had been that the true faith would prevail in open competition with every other doctrine of salvation. Even minor Gahist splinter groups of philosophical and libertarian persuasion were active via American World Net.

We walked on across the bridge and paused at its highest point. From there we could even make out the Great Gate of Prophecy caught in the beam of the pleasure boat's spotlight. Kuhl had been unable to give us any firm information about the risks foreigners ran if they showed their faces in the Goto. Back in Corsica we had read an exclusive report in a German news magazine written by a scoop-seeking journalist who had managed to enter the Blue Dome in disguise. The Goto's reputation as a world-famous chamber of horrors is still founded on memories of the mass mutilation inflicted years ago on a French UN combat patrol. The soldiers in question had penetrated the Goto in armoured cars, looking for a kidnapped International Red Cross official, only to run into an ambush. Captured by Gahist extremists, they were released after weeks of laborious negotiations. Not only had all survived, but, thanks to the excellent medical care they received, the extensive wounds occasioned by the amputation of their noses were healing well.

The spindly arm that insinuated itself between our heads to point out the Great Gate of Prophecy was encased in a skintight sleeve, and we knew that its owner was Freddy even before he addressed us in his nasal version of the city's Piddi-Piddi. When we questioned him about the possibility of touring the Goto, as we immediately did, he told of a method he could recommend. It seemed that a Cyrenian knacker and soap-maker, who had installed a cleverly constructed cubbyhole in his wagon, offered fascinating nocturnal trips through the forbidden quarter when the moon was full and the sky clear. On request, and in return for a small supplement, he would take his passengers to see objects of particular interest. They could even alight and partake of a snack on the Cyrenian soap-maker's houseboat.

We enquired a little more closely into the possibility of driving to certain places. You then asked, point blank, about the former Baptist Mission. Freddy answered you as casually as if it were quite natural that he, being a long-established resident, should be acquainted with particular buildings in the forbidden quarter. After Gahis's third videotaped sermon had condemned the persecution of Christian sects as a necrophilic vice, he said, the American Baptists had seized the opportunity to rent a warehouse overlooking the harbour. This belonged to a group of similar blue-clay buildings which, though clumsily designed and devoid of architectural interest, were extremely ancient. Among the large number of foreign institutions that settled there in the innovative period following the so-called Violet Revolution were the Jehovah's Witnesses and the German government's Goethe Institute. Before two years were up, therefore, the river-port area near the Great Gate of Prophecy was a popular educational and information centre whose uncontrolled activities soon became a thorn in the side of the Gahist radicals.

We accompanied Freddy back to the right bank and followed him down a side street off the boulevard, where the lighting soon became dimmer. Parked in a courtyard was the vehicle he had mentioned, a black, boxlike wagon with two mules harnessed to it. Freddy haggled with the driver in an unintelligible mishmash of Piddi-Piddi and urban dialects, but we did gather that his negotiations took account of our wish to visit the former Baptist Mission. At length the driver opened a skilfully concealed trapdoor and we squeezed through it into the cubbyhole beyond, which contained a padded bench quite big enough for two. When Freddy thrust the upper part of his skinny body through the opening to bid us farewell, we grabbed him under the arms and hauled him inside with a sudden jerk. Gently – almost more gently than anyone would have believed you capable of speaking in our new-found Piddi-Piddi – you told him we valued his company too much to dispense with it. Having drawn apart and sandwiched his struggling form between us, we quelled his resistance by dealing him some well-aimed blows with our elbows. Then we ran our hands over his trunk and lower limbs to make sure the bag of bones didn't have a handgun hidden somewhere under his jacket or overcoat.

20 Melancholy

Seated on deck, I have the forward benches almost to myself. The pleasure boat is only half full. Nearly all the other passengers have chosen to sit down below, where a small buffet has been set up and a loquacious tourist guide is commenting on the sights in advance for the benefit of her charges, a party of Australians. The only people sharing the rancid orange moonlight and cooling breeze with me are a handful of Japanese – possibly the ones I saw arriving at the airport yesterday. Our boat began by travelling upstream for a little way, so as to turn at the confluence of the river and the Egichaean Canal. In so doing, we passed quite close to the city's finest bridge. Built-up throughout its length, it takes the form of a shallow single arch spanning the canal just before it joins the river. Snipers are said to have stationed themselves in the bridge superstructure during the massacre of the Egichaeans. They fired at the heads of individual swimmers and at the small craft in which Egichaean families hoped to escape by river. The snipers were hampered in their work by the countless corpses that had been thrown into the canal in the Egichaean quarter, which were all borne bridgeward by the sluggish current. As ever when the city recalls its horrors, such stories speak of the water being red with the blood of the slain. But even now, in the light of the full moon, I can see how murky it is. Algae thrive hugely on pig effluent, and it's highly improbable that human blood, even in horrendous quantities, could transform dull brown into shimmering red.

When I told Calvin I wanted to acquire a handgun, make immaterial, he contorted his features into an equivocal grin and said I was too late – indeed, I'd always been too late since we first became acquainted. Then, leaving me completely in the dark about my chances, he returned to the two smilers' table. A little later on, when he demanded a substantial sum in new-issue banknotes, I didn't dare to ask – galling though I'd found his tardy response to my request – what I would get for them. I haven't had time until now to see what Calvin has sold me. I get out the package and unwrap the paper to reveal an oily rag which, from its shape, really does contain a small handgun. In a sudden fit of caution I glance over my shoulder and see the Japanese starting to train their camcorders on the right bank. We're nearing the bridge again – that was where we cast off before our turning manoeuvre – but I wait a little longer. I don't unwrap the bundle until we're past it and the Goto is claiming everyone's attention.

The city was renowned for centuries for the skill of its weaponsmiths. Even the museums back home display a few old swords that travelled north-west as spoils of war or merchandise imported via the trade routes of the time. Their new owners considered them so valuable that they withdrew them from use and kept them in their collections, immune from developments in military technology. As times changed, so the city's craftsmen took to making simple firearms. Monstrous great muzzle-loaders from the local workshops remain favourite collectors' pieces to this day, though their claims to lethality are only symbolic, and the elaborately enchased curved daggers manufactured for the domestic and export markets have degenerated into mere ornaments.

My hands are holding a historical hybrid of such curious design that I'm doubtful at first if it could fire a shot at all. It's a pistol whose clumsy twin barrels are mounted one above the other and secured with stout brass bands. The stock, by contrast, is as narrow and short as if made for a very small hand – possibly a woman's, it occurs to me, and I'm briefly touched by the thought that Calvin may have peddled me his personal firearm. Every part of the gun, from its steel, copper, and brass components to the stock of polished horn, is covered with engraved ornamentation. When I succeed after several attempts in breaking the pistol and removing the two cartridges, my fingertips detect that even the chambers are finely engraved. An ardent connoisseur of the city – one who is forever surprising people like me with his erudition – could surely tell me how the extravagant wealth of curlicues on my gun evolved from the characters of various scripts. Freddy would be the right person to translate these engravings into anecdotes.

While I'm almost wistfully recalling Freddy's skill as a storyteller, someone with an American accent tells me what a nice gun I've got. I failed to hear the Jap coming. The ship's diesel engine is loud although we're barely moving.

We're probably going astern against the current so as to drift past the old harbour as slowly as possible. The Japanese introduces himself. I recognize the name – Freddy mentioned it last night in the aromatherapeutic steam room. My memory, which so often fails or deludes me with useless flashes of inspiration, proves hypocritically tractable enough to bring the man's real, American name to my lips. But I say nothing and let him talk. He praises my gun's simple, robust firing mechanism and asks to see a cartridge. It's old, he says – an example of the Western Allies' standardized ammunition for infantry weapons during the Second World War. He's surprised that such a small handgun, which was obviously meant to be concealed on the person, should have been equipped to take such large-calibre ammunition. It's probable, he says, that there was a surplus of that particular ammunition when the gun was made.

We're approaching the Goto's harbour and, consequently, the Great Gate of Prophecy. Our boat's bow-mounted spotlight comes on with an unpleasant snapping sound. At first the beam points straight at the sky, and the particles in the urban smog show the extent of its range. Then, tilting downwards, it lights up the mooring posts projecting from the quay. Some figures are standing there in a group, but still too far away for one to see if they're Cyrenians performing their ritual devotions and ablutions. Although the youth in charge of the spotlight still hasn't managed to focus it on the Great Gate of Prophecy, the bogus Japanese asks me when the famous edifice dates from. I don't reply, wondering whether to tell him instead that it was here on the waterfront that the Great Gahis assembled his most loyal devotees, the Goto's craftsmen and shopkeepers, before marching upstream through the Great Gate of Prophecy to the barracks of the dreaded military police. Legend has it that the Gahists stormed the barrack walls by charging up a ramp composed of their comrades' bullet-riddled bodies. That the Great Gahis was invulnerable to bullets fired by the Impure is another belief that dates back to the storming of the police barracks.

But I don't treat the bogus Japanese to this colourful story. Retrieving the cartridge from his fingers, I insert it in the empty chamber and secrete the weapon in the breast pocket of my jacket. Then I try to look straight at the slit-eyed American's face, which the moonlight has tinged with orange. Having lost the habit of staring at people, I only half succeed: my left eye smarts and begins to water. Despite this I tell my colleague from the New World, my spiritual confrère, his true appellation and once more relish the historical curiosity of his forenames. It seems that, in the United States, nothing is nominally impossible. A military mass murderer's grandson bears the name of the tribe he massacred, and his great-grandson, in perfect innocence, drives a car named after him. I'm told that in my own distant homeland, too, it is now common practice for the names of those who were once slaughtered there on a grand scale to be borrowed in similar fashion.

The man facing me betrays no surprise. He subsists on the same material as I do, so why should he? His features are soft and ill-defined. This is how I like to imagine the US president of the future: a Europoid skull with an Asiatic integument pulled down over it like a latex mask. Beyond him, on the Goto bank, there's a sudden flash: a small, short-lived, very intense white light on a level with the quayside. The dull thud of the impact on our hull does not make itself heard until the flash has faded from my retina, but the dark void of that minimal delay causes the flash in the distance and the thud close at hand to coalesce in the torrid intimacy of cause and effect.

21 Reverence

We had acquired an excellent tourist guide in Freddy. He made another sudden, convulsive attempt to escape from the wagon as it drove off, but a final blow from an elbow caught him – as bad luck would have it – in the face. Although his lower lip swelled up at once, the swelling stopped the bleeding and the good fellow soon overcame the effects of his thick lip sufficiently to deliver a commentary on our entry into the Goto. Eagerly, he leant to left and right in turn so as to give us an equal share of information about what was to be seen through the fine wooden grille in the little door of our cubbyhole. A vast multitude seemed to be circulating in the Goto's narrow alleyways – a hive of nocturnal activity rendered even more crowded, urgent, and dynamic by the absence of any street lighting. Most of the men wore the Gahist costume of which isolated examples had caught our eye in the boulevard. Many youths were also dressed in white, which lent their whole appearance a remarkable element of gravitas.

Freddy explained how the various groups could be distinguished from one another by minor features such as the fall of the trousers or the lack of visible seams. Although the Great Gahis himself had never expressly insisted on the wearing of white, his canticles contained several strongly approving references to that colour, or absence of colour, which to him was symbolic of disinterested purity. In the heyday of Gahism, said Freddy, the white robe was donned only for two sacred activities: religious worship and battle. This was how it had once achieved worldwide fame on television: as the blood-spattered combat gear worn by raiding parties and suicide squads or a white speck in a white expanse of silent, serried worshippers. However, all the video recordings of Gahists at their devotions had been made in the auditorium of the Polytechnic and spanned a brief period only, the time of the Violet Revolution, so Freddy advised us to be wary of them. It was probable that those widely disseminated clips, none of which had a soundtrack, afforded no real idea of the nature of such gatherings. Some peculiar rituals had grown up in the *ognums*, the Gahists' places of worship, during their many years of suppression. The congregations' singing was said to have been incomparably fine – beguilingly sensual, soaringly polyphonic, and intoxicating in its spontaneous melismata and glissandi. Freddy said he hoped with all his heart that a recording of this collective art form had survived. These days, all the city's *ognums* were deserted or had even been degraded for use in some other capacity. Gahis's last, videotaped sermon, his darkly prophetic appearance on television, contained an express ban on the sacred gatherings that had once been held in them and all the rites associated therewith. If credence could be given to the report of a journalist who claimed to have smuggled himself into the Blue Dome in disguise, even that massive

144

rotunda in the heart of the Goto was once more being used as a warehouse, just as it had been during the city's long, humiliating years under foreign rule.

Freddy, who must have noticed that we were enjoying his knowledgeable dissertations, tried to interest us in visiting our driver's home. The Cyrenians were renowned for their fish dishes, he told us. On nights when the moon was full, whole families gathered round huge copper cauldrons to partake of them. Freddy started to list some choice ingredients and spices, but you cut him short and made it clear that we wanted to head straight for the building that had housed the American Baptist Mission. According to Kuhl, the diligent Christians were granted two years there before being compelled to quit the Goto minus their electronic hardware and one or two severed noses. Freddy transmitted our request to the driver through a plastic tube that ran from our cubbyhole to his seat up front. We turned off down a narrow, precipitous street, and suddenly, on your side, the Great Gate of Prophecy came into view above the flat roofs of some low, windowless buildings. Resuming the thread of his discourse, Freddy informed us that the clumsy, unadorned edifice, the only colonnaded building in the world to be constructed of timber and mud alone, had for centuries borne the prosaic name 'Fish Gate', this being where the river fishermen's catches were inspected for freshness and taxed by the authorities of the day. The harbour gate had not acquired its new name until our own time, when it became the jumping-off point for that unparalleled act of self-sacrifice, the Gahists' legendary attack on the central barracks of the military police.

Freddy could now point out the building we sought across a deserted, roughly paved square. It was one of a group of dark, narrow warehouses glinting like anthracite in the moonlight. The driver's voice issued from the plastic tube, and Freddy, interpreting, told us that he was going to make for the riverward side of the buildings, where it would be possible for us to enter without attracting attention. We saw as we drove along them that the side that backed on to the river had latterly been regarded as the front. Damaged facia boards still hung from the walls, and the complete names of firms and organizations could sometimes be deduced from the surviving letters and syllables, pictograms and logos. The big display windows which these firms had self-assertively carved out of the ground-floor walls had later been boarded over, possibly during a final, defensive phase. Our driver steered his wagon so close to the building that we heard the wheel hubs scrape the mud brick. Through the grille of the right-hand window we saw him jump down from his box and push the soot-blackened door open. The doorway was immediately opposite our own little door, with the result that we could step straight from his conveyance into the former premises of the American Baptist Mission, briefly glimpsing only a thin strip of night sky as we did so.

'Other people stink.' We're both fond of jocularly misusing our former unarmed combat instructor's motto on all kinds of appropriate and inappropriate occasions. But our shaven-headed old mentor, wearer of the supreme black belt and highly qualified by his participation in anti-terrorist assignments on three continents, was always in deadly earnest when he uttered his favourite saying. To him, the critical moment or watershed in any hand-to-hand struggle came when one scented an opponent's person. When two adversaries were evenly matched, he said, inhalation of the enemy's aroma determined which of them got a firm grip on the other's laryngeal cartilage. The animal stench that assailed us on entering the old warehouse was simultaneously sweet and acrid. Freddy fell silent, and the Cyrenian knacker, who must have been used to bad smells, pulled out a handkerchief and clamped it over his nose and mouth. Only flesh in the final stages of decay can give off such effluvia, and anyone whose occupation or misfortune has acquainted him with their full abundance will take a different view of the flavour of dried ham or the scent of his beloved's nocturnal breath.

The smell may have been generated by scraps of rotting fish or the corpse of one of the big river rats whose meat, when fresh and skilfully prepared, is said to resemble venison in taste. Our driver, who had switched on a flashlight of modest power, showed us the way to some stairs leading to the floor above. The tall, narrow windows on the first floor admitted so much moonlight that it was possible to look around outside the flashlight's beam as well. The floor was littered with smashed office furniture and the remains of the telecommunications equipment that went with it. Monitors, keyboards, scanners, printers, and many objects whose original function could no longer be discerned – all had been reduced to incredibly small fragments of plastic and alloy. The stairs to the second or top floor had been barricaded with overturned filing cabinets. When the

Cyrenian shone his flashlight on this barrier in a vain attempt to find a way past it, we saw that some of the treads had been smashed, possibly with sledgehammers. And so, having confined our search for useful clues to the first floor, we eventually found a sizeable scrap of printed paper. Freddy read us what was on it and translated the opening lines. He said he recognized the text although it had been rendered into Zeushene after a fashion and with the aid of a phonetically dubious transcriptive system – more precisely, into its chief dialect, which had never, and with good reason, succeeded in becoming a literary language. The fragmentary text came from one of St Paul's epistles. We looked for further clues, knelt amid the debris, turned over smashed drawers, and rummaged bare-handed among shiny bits of scrap metal, fragments of platinum dangling from copper wires like grains of soil clinging to root fibres.

We should have surveyed the room at eye level right away. The extent of the destruction had prompted us to lower our gaze too quickly. You discovered the installation when you straightened up and stretched your limbs, which were stiff from crouching down. It was hanging on the wall opposite the windows, the left-hand side illuminated by a shaft of moonlight. You took the driver's flashlight from him, and we silently examined the large object at close range. At length Freddy said we were looking at a product of contemporary folk art, one of the spontaneous sculptural assemblages of which many examples, never entirely ident-ical but always symbolically similar, had been made at the height of the popular disturbances. When you lifted it down and passed it round, we all found it heavy to hold. It consisted of two lengths of timber of equal thickness but unequal length, the wood being carefully sanded but otherwise untouched. Freddy asserted that crosses of this type were perfectly in keeping with the hidebound, almost boorishly pigheaded missionary zeal of the American churches. And, sure enough, on the back of the cross we found an oval aluminium plate bearing the name and address of a factory for mentally deficient Christian woodworkers in Seattle, Washington.

The plain wooden cross had not been overlooked by those who looted the mission's headquarters. That they deliberately exempted it from the wholesale destruction was apparent from the changes it had undergone. Neatly cut out and thumbtacked to the front was a press cutting. The paper was smooth and firm, the colours seemed only slightly faded. Probably taken from the cover of a news magazine, the photograph was of the last US president. He was depicted with his arms spread wide, perhaps during an election campaign or when leaving his jet at the start of a state visit, before his feet touched foreign soil. Although his paper figure was naturally far too small relative to the massive baulk of timber for him to represent Christ Crucified, the Gahists intent on redecorating the ravaged mission after their own fashion had hit on another idea: they inverted the cross. The longer end of the beam was pointing upward, so America's *numero uno* was hanging upside down, a position in which his celebrated, teeth-baring smile, which had lent him an aura of youthful vigour throughout his two terms of office, acquired a look of brutal prescience. It was as if his beaming face already bore an announcement of the untimely death that would horrify the world.

22 Joy

The pleasure boat is sinking. She's listing to starboard as the crew and passengers clamber over the rail on to the landing stage. The jagged hole torn by the direct hit is already submerged. There were casualties down below. Unconscious or in shock, they're lying on some blankets which the crew have spread out on the jetty. An elderly Australian sits up and starts shouting in a bewildered fashion. The tourist guide and a fellow Australian compel him to lie back and try to calm him down. The quayside was deserted when our boat approached it, listing heavily, and scraped her way along the side. The harbour square – the whole of the unevenly paved expanse between us and the columns of the Great Gate of Prophecy – looks as if the moonlight has swept it clean. No one is threatening us, no one hurrying to our assistance. The captain, his face a monochrome orange, is yelling into a tiny mobile phone. He must be very pale for his features to reflect the moon's colour so faithfully. The help he's requesting would have to come by water, but what boat owner would voluntarily put in at the Goto after what has happened to us?

The bogus Japanese is hovering beside me. When he asks what I think should be done, an irresistible laugh bubbles up in my throat. My self-control is utterly destroyed by its pressure, its titillation, and the spasmodic explosions it brings in its train. In view of our awkward predicament, I must present a peculiar spectacle as I stand there writhing and shaking with mirth. After all, no one can be expected to know that it's years since I laughed so wholeheartedly. My left eye is smarting and watering badly, but my right eye sees the captain deposit his mobile phone on the stump of a mooring post. The tourist guide plucks at his sleeve and leads him over to the old Australian, who, having lustily screamed with pain a moment before, is now breathing stertorously through foam-flecked lips and preparing to die. Still giggling, I totter over to the mooring post and pick up the phone. Slit-Eye follows, and I've a feeling he has great hopes of me.

The captain's mobile is a Luxor. Via the Luxor network it should with luck be possible to get through to someone on the clapped-out urban phone system. I key in the first nine digits and hear the plaintive sound of the satellite exchange's busy tone. Without severing the connection I key in the number again – a simple trick that used to help in the past. Radio contact is maintained. Next, I key in the code number of the old military network and am promptly answered by a mechanical clatter. It was Freddy who drew my attention to this telephone system, which the occupying power installed in the sewers independently of the municipal telephone company's overhead cables. Though not very extensive, the network is robust and has been little used since the revolution. The bogus Japanese, who is now breathing down my neck, listens in as a shrill whistle tells me I've successfully completed the third stage and accessed the ordinary urban system. I key in my own number.

A series of sonorous, almost klaxonlike hoots. This, I know, is what one should hear when calling a number in the rag-boilers' quarter. The same sound once issued from the phone in my room at the Esperanza when I spent an entire afternoon vainly calling the previous tenant of my house, the Italian photographer. A crisp click. For one sobering moment I feel sure I've been cut off, but then I hear a loud 'Hello!' Lieschen has picked up. At an early stage in our life together I forbade her to answer the phone. I receive so few calls, however, that this ban could be neither consistently observed nor blatantly violated. Slit-Eye gathers that I've got through, and the avid expectancy flickering on his face betrays the intensity of his fear and the effort he's making to conceal it. Lieschen guesses who is on the other end of the line even before it occurs to me to say my name. Curtly and succinctly, she asks the relevant questions. I tell her where I am, but just as I'm about to explain the nature of the emergency that has stranded me on the Goto's jetty I detect a change in the white noise on the line. I call to Lieschen, bark out a stuttering hello-hello in Piddi-Piddi followed by one or two softer, drawling hellos in my mother tongue, but we've been cut off, and all my subsequent attempts to get through to my own number are in vain. Eventually the captain relieves me of the phone and has another try himself. He keys in a number at top speed, plugging his right ear with his forefinger because the dying Australian has started to scream once more – remarkably loudly.

I walk upstream along the quay. The bogus Japanese doesn't budge from my side. He must have heard Lieschen's voice and thinks our brief conversation is a guarantee of assistance. His faith in me is clearly stronger than his herd instinct. Either that, or the dying Australian's screams are propelling him, like me, out of earshot. I put on speed, but he dogs my footsteps and asks if we can escape from the Goto by following the course of the river. I don't reply. As quickly as I can without breaking into a run, I hurry toward the warehouses bordering the harbour square. This was where presumptuous Westerners made their deepest inroads into the city. UNESCO proclaimed the Goto a World Heritage site and promptly opened an office there. Other international do-gooders moved in nearby. Unwilling to be left out, my native Germany rented the last vacant floor in the former warehouses, and our cultural institute installed itself immediately above the American Baptist Mission. There followed a limited amount of business activity, one or two courses in commercial German, and a series of English-language lectures delivered by German experts on administrative law. A friendly was arranged with the Juniors, Germany's national football team, but had to be cancelled because of civil unrest. The old warehouses beside the harbour were among the first places where xenophobic disturbances broke out. The city's security services held back, and the foreign cultural organizations' security guards, though well paid and heavily armed, were numerically too weak to prevent the buildings from being stormed. The looters' spoils were on sale in the city's markets in the days that followed. One entire wall in

Freddy's office is lined with video cassettes, a fine collection of French, Italian, American, and even Russian films in their original versions – all of them stolen goods which he managed to acquire at bargain prices.

The short walk to the warehouses is doing me good. For some time now, I've been suffering from a circulatory disorder affecting the toes of my right foot. They only warm up and transmit more than a faint, prickling sensation at Freddy's Steam Bath, when I alternate between the steam rooms and the plunge pool. At least they're hurting now, and I note with satisfaction that my companion is in even greater pain. He seems to be limping. Perhaps one of his pointed black patent leather shoes is pinching him, or he may have twisted his ankle on the uneven surface. He finally grasps that I'm making for one of the old warehouses and asks what I have in mind. Matching his American accent, I tell him I'm looking for the Goethe Institute. He asks who 'Gerty' was, but instead of treating him to an explanation I quicken my step again. Both the entrances on the harbour side have been boarded up with rough-hewn planks. In a fit of animosity I pretend I'm trying to get in and rattle them furiously. Then I hurry past the building next door to a narrow passageway leading to the front of the warehouses.

The soot-stained door is unlocked as usual. I omit to warn my companion about the darkness that engulfs us when it closes, or about the stench that makes my gorge rise despite my many visits to the building in recent years. I hurry up the stairs. Their minor hazards – broken treads, gaps in the banisters – have long ceased to delay me. Once in the Baptist Mission's erstwhile offices on the first floor I turn and see, by the moonlight streaming through the high windows, that my bogus Japanese is anxiously but not unskilfully groping his way up the dark staircase. The fixtures and fittings on the first floor have been smashed to pieces with extreme thoroughness, and access to the top floor seems to be denied by an impenetrable barricade of heavy metal cabinets piled on top of each other. But the route to the Goethe Institute does, in fact, run through one such filing cabinet, the back of which has been converted into a secret door. The stairs beyond are in darkness, and several of them are missing. I can't wait to hear my moon-faced American's startled cry as he treads on thin air, but he follows me up on all fours and is fortunate and perceptive enough to cross the yawning void unscathed.

All the windows in the former Goethe Institute have been boarded up and additionally draped with thick blankets to cover any chinks through which the glow from the screen might escape. I've no idea who else uses the room and its data transmission terminal. Whenever I want to send a message to the old country, Freddy books me a slot. The terminal is then reserved for me for three hours – far longer than I need, but it's allegedly impossible to rent it for a shorter period and a smaller fee. The Cyrenian knacker who drives me to the Goto in his converted mule wagon seldom has to wait outside for longer than half an hour.

The electronics are concealed beneath the floorboards, nine sections of which can be individually removed. An aluminium sheet folds back, enabling the monitor and PC to be lifted out of the floor by means of a scissor mechanism. I've already accessed American World Net by the time the bogus Japanese crawls into the glow from the screen, still on all fours and bleeding profusely from a cut on the forehead. Although my colleague has missed the best part, logistically speaking, the screen is still showing the introductory graphics: a gigantic wooden cross that seems to glide past a globe rotating on its own axis to the strains of the American national anthem, as if the crude object were surfing the atmosphere of our blue planet. As usual, I click on one of the five ecumenical discussion forums, in this instance the Round Table for Apocalypse and Prophecy. I signal my wish to take part by entering one of my code names. I call myself Egichaeus as a rule, though I sometimes use an Egichaean distortion of the name of one of Christ's disciples. Today I shall access the electronic forum as the Apostle of Love, whose name the Egichaeans shorten to a single syllable. After hovering over the keyboard, my fingers swiftly type what I've learned from my last pneumatic post transmission. For the benefit of the authorities at home I predict some small part of what will happen in the next few hours, on the ninth anniversary of Gahis's death. My valiant colleague is peering over my shoulder, breathing heavily. For once, so as to give him some food for thought, I type my report in English. Here in the worldwide playground of esoteric crackpots and religious scatterbrains, encryption is unnecessary. Any secret and, consequently, any future occurrence is concealed in this great uproar, this hubbub created by prophets of salvation and damnation, like a seed germinating in the warmth of a dunghill.

23 Fun

Freddy was a gem, and we found the time to polish him thoroughly. Our nocturnal exit from the Goto was a protracted process. The streets were busier now, and our wagon could negotiate them only at a walking pace. Freddy had grown still more nervous since our fruitless visit to the Baptist Mission. As if he felt to blame for this failure and wanted to atone for it, he proceeded – overeagerly – to tell us about the history of Gahism and kept trying to divert our gaze to the nocturnal bustle outside. Half on your lap with his nose to the grille, he started to explain the modern origin of an archaic-looking pilgrim's costume, but you gently thrust him back between us. We took hold of his long, slender hands, cracked his knuckles for him, and questioned him about the foreigners living in the city. You reminded him of his boast on the terrace of the Esperanza: that his steam bath was a favourite rendezvous for foreigners. Although he denied knowing Spaik for a long time, it occurred to him, when you deftly dislocated the little finger of his right hand, that a German of that name was one of his steam bath's most faithful customers. The man not only patronized his establishment every other night at least but tended to remain there till dawn, and it was more

158

than possible that we would find him at the steam bath if
we went there as soon as we left the Goto. Being suspicious
of Freddy's readiness to engineer an immediate encounter
with Spaik, we took the time to enquire more closely into
Spaik's circumstances. All our patience notwithstanding,
we were eventually obliged to dislocate the little finger of
Freddy's left hand as well before he would divulge Spaik's
address. It seemed that he lived in the so-called rag-boilers'
quarter, an old artisans' district on the other side of the
boulevard from the river.

Freddy's interrogation proved so engrossing, we failed to
notice that we'd left the Goto behind. Our attention was
only redirected to the outside world by the noise in Freedom of Speech Boulevard. Our conveyance pulled up at the
kerb. Getting out, we paid the Cyrenian neither more nor
less than Freddy had recommended. The moon had set by
now, and the boulevard was bright with a mixture of artificial lighting. The dim, yellowish glow shed by the
concrete street lights dating from the occupation was in
ludicrous contrast to their imposing height and would have
illuminated little more than a modest circle round their
clumsy bases, but the boulevard's shopkeepers had added
rows of lamps of their own at a later stage. Strung on steel
cables that brushed pedestrians' heads at many points was
a hotchpotch of very disparate light sources. You particularly liked the numerous gas lamps, with their blindingly
white incandescent mantles and multicoloured glass
shades. But the electric lights were more heterogeneous
still. It was as if every municipal council in the world, when
replacing its street lights, had sent one discarded specimen

to Freedom of Speech Boulevard to be displayed there like an exhibit in an open-air museum.

We stood on the edge of the pavement, trying to flag down a taxi. There was hardly a gap in the traffic in either direction, but it flowed with surprising speed. We stepped back from the kerb whenever a truck or a bus bore down on us in the right-hand lane. Numerous taxis passed us too, but the drivers of the few that weren't already taken ignored our signals. It eventually occurred to you that Freddy, whose sagging form we were supporting between us, might be mistaken for a drunk. We released his elbows and told him to hail a taxi himself. Sure enough, he elicited a reaction from the very next one, a bulbous beast of an ancient American limousine. The driver performed a risky manoeuvre: he braked abruptly and swerved into the right-hand lane. Heeling over hard, the monster mounted the high kerb. It escaped from the traffic in a shower of sparks, gently nudged aside a melon seller's handcart, and came to rest in the midst of pedestrians and stallholders.

Our drive to the rag-boilers' quarter, which we spent chatting with Freddy, passed quickly. Having sagged between us in the boulevard as though bereft of all resilience, he blossomed once more on the taxi's leatherette seat. We had no further need to question him. His narrative flow was boosted by every interested glance, every friendly nod, every marvelling shake of the head. And when he at last broke into German – we were in a dark, narrow street temporarily blocked by an overturned motor-scooter taxi, a so-called *vuspi* – it was as if the city's Piddi-Piddi and our own native tongue were good neighbours whose boundaries it was permissible to cross without more ado. Freddy spoke German with singular rapidity – faster, undoubtedly, than we had ever heard it spoken before. He could elide syllables in such a way that they became fused into consonantal clicks or grunts. And yet, despite the acceleration to which his words were subjected, they very seldom lost their original sound.

Freddy told us of his early days in the city. He had evidently been sent to the area as the vanguard of a major German industrial concern, his immediate task being to reconnoitre the perilous but promising terrain and establish a preliminary bridgehead for the firm's plenipotentiary-to-be. He rhapsodized about his time as a new arrival at the Esperanza. The hotel had then been in the throes of a kind of gold-rush fever. Madame Haruri, the manageress, was a paragon of urban femininity. Her height inordinately accentuated by immense high heels, she paid nightly visits to the bar to drink and swap banter with businessmen and agents from all over the world. He himself – he begged us to believe him – had been a heavyweight in those days, a young man superabundantly endowed with body-builder's muscle, not adipose tissue. What was more, this erstwhile Freddy had performed a memorable feat of endurance in the bar one night. Alone among many challengers, he had managed to defy Madame Haruri for a considerable time at *givuk*, a form of arm-wrestling. It was six whole minutes before the hotel manageress forced his wrist on to the bar counter by dint of her physical strength and murderous twisting technique. In the wonderfully hysterical world of the Esperanza, his stamina had promptly earned him the nickname 'The Cast-Iron Kraut'. However, the immediate consequence of this local renown had been his provisional recall from the city. His departmental chief, a man who, though still young like himself, had already caught a bad cold from the chill breath of expediency, promptly transferred him to Malta and put him on ice for safety's sake. From there, half Maltese and terribly emaciated after six months' exile, he returned to the city to make a fresh start. By setting up his steam bath he had created an ideal base of operations from which to help and advise his successor as the firm's chief representative, who had now been long established in the city.

Our willingness to listen to Freddy's effusions waned when we turned into the street where Spaik was said to be living. All Freddy knew, so he claimed, was that Spaik had rented one of the old rag-boilers' houses there. Unfortunately, nearly every building in the long, narrow street, which twisted and turned like a maze, seemed once to have been used for paper manufacture. The passers-by whom Freddy questioned on our behalf gave facetious responses of which most, if we understood them correctly, implied that remembering a foreigner's face was injurious to one's health. Either that, or they flatly stated that foreigners changed their appearance so completely from day to day that they all ended up looking like the same stranded outsider. So we drove up and down the street a few times until it struck you that, unlike his ceaselessly wagging tongue, Freddy's eyes had come to rest twice – on the same house.

We had reached our destination. You paid a horrendous fare and even rounded it up with a suitably excessive tip. Then we dragged Freddy, struggling feebly, over to the building betrayed by his telltale gaze. It was two-storeyed, with shutters over the ground-floor windows. A lamp hung from a bracket over the door. A chromium-plated shade directed the harsh light from a mercury vapour bulb down on to us and good old Freddy's haggard face. Sweat coated it like a film of lubricating oil, and he was now talking at an unsurpassable rate. His German was on the verge of degenerating into an unintelligible twitter.

How nice and refreshing it is to look past that picture of misery and see you standing there. Time and the exigencies of an Enforcement Branch mission can wait while I feast my eyes on you. The piece of jewellery your hand discovered on the back seat of the taxi can now be seen to full advantage. Just for fun, you let me put it round your neck in the dim interior. A previous passenger, doubtless a local beauty, must have mislaid it there. Now, in the mordant glare outside Spaik's front door, I perceive that the intricate pendant, a species of necklace, has been fashioned from the innards of electronic devices. Its delicate filigree of wires, resistors, and miniature diodes and transistors form a glittering kaleidoscope of polished precious metals and multifarious enamels. Letters and numerals can be seen on the diminutive metal cylinders and rectangles. Seduced by their aesthetic charm, one could almost believe that these components, which once performed a data-processing function, have an equally meaningful role to fulfil in their new, craftsman-determined setting. I'm so entranced by the sight of your bejewelled appearance that I scarcely seem to hear Freddy jabbering away like self-dissolving submusic, like a kind of muzak.

24 Rapture

Spaik's front door isn't locked. We thrust Freddy into a
gloomy passage. A door leads to the ground-floor rooms,
a steep flight of stairs to the floor above. The little house is
silent, dark, and musty. Before exploring it further we must
jettison unwanted ballast. You propel Freddy to the end of
the passage, where a small, faintly luminous window
signals the presence of a back door. It admits the three of us
to an enclosed courtyard. This is large, square, and empty
save for three low, circular troughs. We let Freddy walk on
ahead, muttering to himself. You use the distance between
you to take a little run and high-kick him in the back. He
teeters in front of one of the stone troughs. He's still
speaking, but his voice has lost all its strength. It's little
more than a whisper now, but you and I, in a detached but
affecting manner, detect the familiar quality in this breathy,
sibilant sound. Our eyes meet. I'm sure we're thinking of
the same thing: of our basic telecommunications training,
of those signals exercises in the Nevada desert, of those
long nights in front of our radio sets, of the sensation in
our throats and hearts, initially tentative, then choking and
ultimately tear-jerking, when there issued from our headsets, from the babble of voices over the long wave, from the

quacking and chattering of foreign languages, a snatch of good old German.

Freddy stares into the circular trough as though conversing with the thistles growing there. A punch in the back of the neck sends him sprawling over the lip. He rolls over on his back and presents us with a view of his face, which has been badly scratched by the prickly undergrowth. His lips move, trying to tell the world something. Whatever it is, it's far too faint for any ear to catch. With a few kicks, the very simplest ones in the unarmed combat manual, we give our compatriot all that's required to silence him for good. His teeth, his skull and bones, so meagrely upholstered with fat and muscle, snap loud and clear in the nocturnal air. Then absolute silence falls. Not even the sound of the traffic in the boulevard, which was audible as a distant roar outside in the street, carries to this inner courtyard.

We turn to face Spaik's little house. All the windows overlooking the courtyard are closed and in darkness. We re-enter the passage and wait awhile, but nothing stirs. Then we go up to the door leading to the ground-floor rooms. It isn't locked. You grope for a light switch and, after flickering briefly, a monumental neon tube dispenses a white glare. The two rooms, which we take in at a glance, are connected by a wide passage. All the windows have been carefully rendered lightproof with black plastic sheeting and adhesive tape. It is clear that the rooms serve one purpose only: in the middle of the larger of the two is a wooden table bearing a television set, a video recorder, and a CD player. Surveying this ensemble and the bare, brightly lit room, we're involuntarily reminded of a regular workplace. On the other hand, the floor beneath the chair and table is strewn with trampled tablets, and the empty *zuleika* bottles and numerous crumpled tissues lying on the floorboards are suggestive less of work than of the unsavoury habits of a lonely old recluse. We examine the video cassettes on the table. To our surprise, they're merely Gahis's nine videotaped sermons, the versions subtitled in Piddi-Piddi and so warmly recommended to us by Dr Zinally. You remove one of the cassettes from its well-worn cover and start to insert it in the VTR, but I dissuade you with a shake of the head from giving us a sight of the tape, which has clearly been played a great deal.

Gahis is present here in any case, though in a simpler and technologically older form. Hanging on the wall is a poster, a black and white photograph reproduced on imitation canvas. But for the caption in big, florid, pseudo-oriental lettering, we should never have guessed that the subject was the Prophet of the Revolution himself. The photograph shows a young man, bare-chested and tolerably good-looking, seated behind a desk. His shoulders are slender, his arms exceedingly muscular. Balanced on his hands is a martial weapon, a broad-bladed knife resembling a machete. As though to nullify this warlike impression, the Great Gahis is wearing a necklace, a chain whose delicate links are poorly defined.

You stroke the Prophet's muscular chest with the tip of your forefinger, and it perceptibly yields under your touch. I take the poster down, revealing the cavity beyond: a brick-lined niche almost as big as the sheet that concealed it. This niche, which extends far into the wall, houses an installation that mystifies us. Protruding from above is a tube as thick as a man's arm, the mouth being secured by an elaborate brass and aluminium flap mechanism. A stout hose connects the mouth of the tube to a gas cylinder with a valve that clearly serves to regulate the pressure. Encircling the valve are three knurled copper rings. These bear numerals and can be turned in opposing directions. They remind you of old-fashioned mechanical time clocks. You're probably right: the valve rings enable a time to be set, but that brings us no nearer to elucidating the contraption's overall function and true purpose.

On the ledge below the apparatus are three steel cylinders a good nine inches long, their diameter suggesting that they would fit into the tube. We unscrew them all. Two are empty, but the third contains a strip of black rubber with white writing on it: a single sentence in German. You read it aloud, shaking your head. It baldly states, in formal language, that the unnamed correspondent is terminating his information service forthwith and for good. The handwriting is schoolboyishly neat, and its surfeit of curlicues and flourishes tells us that the writer must have learned it long before our own days in primary school. The short text is studded with spelling mistakes. The word 'information', for example, is so garbled that we guess rather than read it. You roar with laughter at our discovery. Jocularly, you liken the whole arrangement to a pneumatic post terminal. You even improve on the joke by hazarding that, in future, Spaik intends to send his remarkable reports home by this equally remarkable means.

Our search of the remainder of the ground floor proves

more difficult. Although the second room is adequately lit by the first, it's crammed with musty old junk: piles of furniture, discarded television sets, empty suitcases, mounds of clothes, stacks of old newspapers and periodicals. It's as if the unwanted effects of some former tenant have at some stage been stored here and forgotten. We take the trouble to look through the printed matter. This falls into three categories: several years' issues of a New York magazine devoted to art photography, various Italian sports journals, and some bizarre local publications – photo romances with balloon texts in Piddi-Piddi. We marvel at these curious novelettes. They bear titles such as *Sweet Emotion* or *Tender Feelings,* and the covers invariably depict young couples in languishing poses. The lovers whose tribulations are recounted in pictures always sport Western clothes and modern hairstyles, whereas the subsidiary characters – the future married couple's relations, opponents, and rivals – are branded as locals by their traditional attire. Having leafed through a dozen of these photo romances backwards, you find our supposition confirmed: they all end with a full-page wedding picture in which guests in regional costume surround a bride in white and a tailcoated bridegroom.

None of this has any bearing on Spaik. Impatiently, we go on rummaging. We come across the frame and tyres of a bicycle, once a far from inexpensive semi-racer. Right at the back, behind a mattress propped against the wall, is a long plastic sack. We rip open the black PVC and are surprised to find that it contains a mummified corpse, much reduced in weight by desiccation. We haul it out into a better light. It appears to have belonged to a man who died wearing a pair of striped flannel pyjamas. The fabric is remarkably well preserved. The mummy's mouth is wide open, and the tongue, which has shrivelled to a gnarled point, is jutting from it vertically. On the forefinger of the right hand is an exceptionally broad gold band inset with a triangular stone. The finger snaps when you pull off the ring and disintegrates into its constituent ossicles, together with dust and particles of fibre. You blow away the residue of tissue and discover some lettering engraved inside the ring: a date and a short word, probably a name. Unfortunately, the gold was so worn away during the wearer's lifetime that the numerals and letters can no longer be clearly distinguished. The engraved name begins with a 'P'. You slip the ring on to your left hand; it not only fits you but suits you as well. I myself can see how admirably the two pieces of jewellery go together, the dead man's ring and the necklace you found in the taxi. They might be accessories common to a local fashion which you have nonchalantly chosen to adopt as a matter of course, and not for one night only.

We climb the steep wooden stairs to the first floor and soon become convinced that these are Spaik's actual living quarters. Plugged into the front of the television set in the larger room, which seems to be a kind of living room, is a *German Fun* decoder – one of the earliest series, whose electronics were still housed in a clumsy Walkman case. Drawn right up to the television set is a huge, incomparably hideous armchair of thin woven reed. When we sit down in it together for a moment, just for fun, I notice that the floor between the chair and the TV is littered with fragments of glass, clearly the remains of a bottle of shaving lotion. Gingerly kneeling down, you sniff these fragments and the small round table on which the TV stands, but if any shaving lotion was spilt there its scent has long since evaporated. The room beyond is Spaik's bedroom. Trodden into the cracks between the floorboards beside the bed are a multitude of coloured tablets. You turn back the bedclothes with your fingertips. Spaik seems to be a quiet sleeper, because the mattress displays a narrow but deep indentation. The sheet there is yellow and in many places brown. Overcome with impotent disgust at such indescribable squalor, we each spit on it in turn.

But we take as much trouble as before. We slit open the mattress and the cushion of the television chair, search the sparse furniture, feel in every pocket of Spaik's unsightly, neglected garments. At some stage it strikes you that there's not a scrap of paper up here: not a newspaper, not a book, not a letter, not a memo. We fail to find even a sales slip among Spaik's belongings. Arrayed on a shelf above the television set are some of the same metal cylinders we came across downstairs in the niche behind Gahis's photoportrait. Each contains a piece of rubber or plastic with writing on it. The text is always couched in German, two or three almost meaningless sentences referring to notification, information, or data transmission. Much of the spelling is so faulty that we can't be sure we've understood the text correctly. In one of the cylinders we discover a scrap of paper, apparently a bottle label. The bottle it once adorned contained a beverage entitled 'Genuine Old Zuleika Brandy'. The back is inscribed in pencil. The same handwriting, but its traces are too smudged to be legible. It looks as if an abecedarian endeavouring to decipher the words has run his forefinger over them again and again. Replacing the cylinders on the shelf, we know what next to look for. The walls are bare save for a faded tapestry. You pull it down, and behind it is a tube terminal like the one on the ground floor. The tube emanates from below. Embedded almost vertically in the wall, it clearly does no more than link the two floors.

That leaves the wooden ladder leading to the hatchway in the ceiling. It's old and looks rather rickety. I station myself beneath it and support the uprights. You slip off your shoes and cautiously proceed to climb, but one of the rotten rungs snaps under your weight when you brace your neck and shoulders against the flap, which is jammed. Some white stuff, powdery and friable as dried bird shit, comes raining down. You stick your head through the opening and look around while I watch you from below. Your new necklace swings out towards me. You make an odd impression, as if you'd ascended Jacob's ladder and thrust your head, by main force, into some supernal realm. It seems to take your eyes a while to get used to the gloom in the roof space. At length you call down that there's nothing much to be seen. The roof space is empty, filthy, and only waist-high – unworthy of closer inspection.

That means we've seen everything. We turn out the lights. All that remains is to wait for the old man. You go to one of the windows overlooking the street and open it a crack. Cool air streams in. The night has only now, shortly before a new dawn, sloughed off the heat of the preceding day. It's utterly still outside. Even the boulevard seems to have quietened down. No roar of traffic or blaring horns carry to our ears. But then, standing temple to temple in the refreshing current of air, we do hear something after all: a distant clatter that gains in volume, acquiring resonant undertones. We recognize the medley of sounds. It's the harsh percussion of worn-out track, the swelling rattle and screech of decrepit rolling stock – a deplorable noise we've often heard in poorer countries. But this time the familiar phenomenon sounds even worse: the tortured metal howls as if it's about to lose contact with ballast and embankment, to forfeit its earthbound banality. The steel sings as if the train is heading heavenward.

25 Remembrance

The Old Municipal Railway is conveying me home. Never having used it before, I've only now – very belatedly – grasped its advantages. The track runs above street level on cast-iron stilts, and the city's venerable old districts cower beneath its dark rails like victims of rape. Made up of three carriages and a locomotive, our train rattles along quite arbitrarily above pedestrians and donkey carts, *vuspis*, and innumerable pick-ups of Japanese manufacture, as if the railway was from every point of view an earlier life form – as if, during the last few hours of this night that is spawning the ninth anniversary of Gahis's death, some huge prehistoric worm were crawling over the medieval mud-brick buildings and their latter-day inhabitants. The Old Municipal Railway was conceived of as an inner circle by the German engineers who designed it, supervised its construction, and had every nut and bolt transported by sea from their distant homeland. They intended the more modern quarters and outlying suburbs then in process of development to be ringed by another two lines designed for higher speeds. But they never built more than this inner circle, which is really a lopsided oval. Its planned extension was prevented by the hazards of the area, its large- and small-scale wars and frequent *coups d'état*. Thanks to the municipal authorities' chronic lack of funds, the existing railway system has remained unchanged for almost a century. This means that the ornate stations, with their wealth of brass, not only preserve the technological pride of their time of origin but, being shabby and battered, cast scorn on it as well. When the occupying power moved out the Old Municipal Railway was sold to a consortium of Western firms, which planned a thorough renovation of the track and all its technological installations. But anti-Western disturbances and the persistent inaccessibility of the Goto soon put paid to hopes of using the railway for touristic purposes. Work on renovating it, which had already begun, was suspended, and it continued to be run as it had been in previous decades: as a temporary, rattletrap system forever breaking down and forever undergoing makeshift repairs.

Lieschen came to fetch me. Being familiar with the workings of the Old Municipal Railway, she caught a train to the forbidden quarter, found me on the quayside, and took me from there to the Goto's only station. This is situated quite close to the old river port, squeezed like a massive ship's bow between two mud-brick buildings of imposing height. I was amazed that the countless little window panes in the façade, and even the big glass swing doors, were still intact. All have been blackened by decades of soot and frosted by the sand that blows through the city, but the tutelary hand of providence – and also, perhaps, a feeling of awe inspired by the ethos of the building, which has always remained alien – spared them from destruction by machine-gun bursts loosed off during revolutionary firefights or stones hurled by triumphant teenagers.

I'm wearing the disguise Lieschen brought me, which I donned in the shelter of a dark gateway. Known as a *kuud*, the garment is a long cloak of white goat's-hair with a voluminous hood, an old-fashioned pilgrim's costume which has come back into fashion in recent years. The *kuud* may be worn by Gahists who have undertaken a pilgrimage to the northern salt lakes and fasted there for three days on the site of a former detention camp. The Great Gahis is said to have been confined in this labour camp as a very young man. The story goes that he brought off a daring escape and rejoined his forlorn and despairing disciples after trekking for three days and nights attired in a goatherd's cloak. Only when the whole of the little band had assembled round him did he throw back the hood and utter his celebrated dictum about rubbing salt into the national wound.

This legend has its sceptics, even among the Gahists. Information about Gahis's background and early years is meagre and conflicting. The only known photograph dating from his youth shows him seated behind a rough wooden table, stripped to the waist and holding a traditional reed-cutter's knife in both hands. Whether this was a real-life snapshot of him or a piece of symbolic stagecraft is a potentially explosive political and theological question, and may only be raised discreetly if at all. Freddy once whispered to me in the haze of the aromatherapeutic steam room that the *kuud* and all the anecdotes about Gahis's spell as a convict originated in the tailors' shops of the Goto, where pilgrims' robes are manufactured out of goat's-hair felt in the traditional manner and sold for high prices. Freddy maintained that the youthful picture was a montage concocted by an imaginative and technically adept photographer, the scion of a well-known Armenian family, from a snap of an unknown man and a mature portrait of Gahis retouched to make him look younger. It was, he said, a counterfeit head on someone else's torso. One of the city's Purity Committees, an organ of the Gahist judicial system, had detected the resourceful photographer's subterfuge. He was blinded in the left eye and his studio in Freedom of Speech Boulevard shut down, but the picture had already attained such a wide circulation that no one dared to brand it a fake. Reproduced on imitation linen, it now hangs in many stores and workshops, usually near the door and at head height, so that customers can kiss the figure's hands. I also learned from Freddy, who has long contrived to feed me titbits from the city and the world at large, and will doubtless do so in the future, that this revolutionary icon has found its way into Western encyclopedias, or at least into one of their Internet editions.

Also part of the *kuud* costume is something not unlike a surgical mask. It seems that the herdsmen of the salt lakes cover their mouths and noses with a piece of goat's-hair felt to protect the respiratory tract. To the pilgrim, the *kuud* mask signifies that the true believer safeguards himself against evil words and pernicious ideas – against the noxious, wind-borne spiritual emanations that assail him from all quarters. I myself am extremely glad to have tied such a rectangle of cloth over my face on Lieschen's advice, because five shabbily dressed youths, identifiable as Gahists by their narrow white sashes, have boarded our carriage. Seating themselves on the long wooden bench opposite Lieschen and me, they at once proceed to assemble a weapon from the numerous components in the plastic bags they're carrying. Although antiquated, this small mortar of Chinese provenance is popular on account of its indestructibility. One of the bipod's legs, which is missing, has been replaced with a roughly trimmed branch lashed to its stump with masses of wire. The five youngsters quickly agree on how the pieces fit together, saying little. Finally, when the weapon has already been armed with a melon-shaped bomb, one of them taps it all over with a hammer.

Lieschen has been an interested spectator of the mortar's assembly. She even gets up and goes over to the youngsters to point out where a screw has been wrongly inserted, and they readily accept the girl's advice. I've never really fathomed the relative status of the sexes in Gahism. The Blue Dome is said to have contained a shrine dedicated to The Mother, a chest of dark wood in which Gahis's mother's simple jewellery and dog-eared books were preserved. The Prophet's work reputedly embodies a strict doctrine of heredity that attributes all the virtues – and Gahism recognizes martial virtues only – to the maternal genes. On the other hand, no religious community surpasses the Gahists in their abhorrence of menstruation. Some radical splinter groups even hold the smell of decomposing female blood to be lethal. Indeed, if Western press reports are to be believed, women have been accused of murdering their husbands on the strength of this tenet.

Zinally, who regards the Prophet as Darwin's legitimate heir, is an authority on the subject. He says that the super-stitious sectarians' manic fear of menstruation is supported by only one of Gahis's sayings: 'The young wolf fears the blood of the she-wolf.' This dictum is not, of course, to be taken literally, but must be interpreted in the light of the Prophet's bio-historical doctrine.

The young Gahists get out at the first station in the boule-vard. They have difficulty in manoeuvring the mortar's splayed legs through the door. When they finally get the monster outside, one of them sticks his head back into the carriage and bids us all – especially me, the pilgrim – a cordial farewell. He employs an elaborate, old-fashioned phrase of which the last words are drowned by the hiss of the pneumatic doors.

Lieschen must have set off immediately after my call. I, the local foreigner, would not even have known where to find the railway station in the rag-boilers' quarter. She reached the Goto's harbour just as I got back from the Baptist Mission. The crisp click-clack of her orthopaedic boots came echoing across the square as she strode towards me with brisk and resolute tread. The girl looked taller than usual in the moonlight, as if she had shot up like a mushroom in the shadow of my solicitude, the routine of my advancing years. She was vigorously, almost spiritedly, swinging a carrier bag. The plastic must have been pure white, because it had taken on the orange glow of the moon. Lieschen spotted my cut before I could ask her what was in the bag. I had instinctively raised my right hand to my mouth, intending to lick it. She got me to show it to her at once, and it was then that I first saw the gaping wound. The middle joint of my right forefinger had been deeply lacerated. Lieschen deposited her bag on the paving stones and rummaged in it with both hands. I heard the purr of a zip fastener; then she brought out a packet of sticking plasters and a pair of nail scissors.

My hand has only been hurting since Lieschen treated it. Now, in the light of the railway carriage, it brings back memories of my colleague. The moon-faced American's final act was to help me replace the electronics in the floor of the gloomy Goethe Institute. The telescopic mechanism, a practical device but always hard to budge, got stuck for the very first time, and we had to apply concerted, rhythmical pressure on either side to release the joints. Perhaps I should bring some lubricant with me on my next visit, as a precaution against future blockages. This time, at any rate, I was very glad the American had been such a help. We made our way downstairs together. Far more care is essential when descending the treacherous staircase to the Baptist Mission than on the way up. I went on ahead to warn him of the missing treads, then stood aside at the foot and let him precede me. The moon, which was now at a favourable height, sent its broad beams slanting across the wrecked office. Having scanned it with an air of curiosity, my colleague bent over a heap of old floppy disks. I let him get on with it, stirring the debris with the toe of my shoe as if I myself might find something there. He produced some glasses from the breast pocket of his jacket and squatted down to read an inscription. I came up behind him and asked what it said. His reply – doubtless the opening words of a longish sentence – was drowned by the infernal din of my ladies' pistol and, consequently, lost to me and posterity. With great momentum, as if I'd not only shot him in the head but shoved him in the back as well, my colleague fell forwards on to the Baptists' diskettes.

It's only now, in the jolting railway carriage, as I listen to Lieschen's low humming with my painful hand reposing on her plastic carrier bag, that I think to examine the weapon that injured me. I slip my left hand under the hem of the *kuud* and bring it out into the light. I now see what happened: one of the brass bands encircling the superimposed barrels burst when I fired, and the sharp edge pierced the flesh of my trigger finger.

26 Hope

The *kuud* felt agreeably warm round my back and
shoulders, not only in the Goto but just now in the railway
carriage. The city can be unpleasantly chilly in the hours
before dawn, especially when the sky is clear. But now, on
the short walk from the station in the rag-boilers' quarter to
our little house, I'm sweating heavily in my goat's-hair
cloak as I follow Lieschen home. My right foot, which is
hurting more and more, makes it quite impossible to stride
along evenly. It feels numb to the ankle, and the intervals
between the stabbing pains that shoot from my toes to my
knee, via the instep and shin, are becoming ever shorter. I
hobble along two, three, five paces behind Lieschen, who
forges ahead in her orthopaedic footwear as if the black
monsters were weightless – as if it won't be long before she
can dispense with their rigid support. My right hand, too, is
making progress a torment. Although I'm grimly holding it
at shoulder height, my lacerated finger is throbbing like
mad. The blood has long ago seeped through the plaster
and is trickling down my wrist into my sleeve. When we
cross the deserted vegetable market, I call after Lieschen's
fast-receding figure and request a breather.

I go over to the fountain and sit down. Propping my

painful foot on the edge of the basin, I hold out my hand for Lieschen to examine it. First, however, she reaches into her carrier bag and brings out a thick wad of money. I recognize it by the shoelace I used to tie the banknotes together: it's our household emergency reserve. The cash has already come in handy, Lieschen tells me. On the way to the Goto her railway carriage was invaded by three Gahists, grizzled old men but armed with modern automatic weapons. The trio invited her and the only other passenger, a plump young Zeushene, to make a donation in honour of the ninth anniversary of the Great Gahis's death. With some difficulty, she managed to extract all the new five-hundreds from the bundle of banknotes, which was still half frozen, and deposited them in a skinny, outstretched paw. The young Zeushene, however, was foolish enough to contribute a single obsolete ten-thousand, and a very tattered and dirty one at that. As if this were the only possible response, one of the old men riddled the young man's vitals with an entire magazine from his automatic weapon. Watching from the window of the train as it pulled out, Lieschen saw them dump him on the platform and board a train going in the opposite direction.

Lieschen has never, as far as I can recall, spoken to me at such length before. She may have done so to take my mind off her ministrations to my finger. And indeed, while listening I haven't felt her remove the blood-soaked plaster. Obviously intending to make a more elaborate job of the wound this time, she has laid out all she needs on the edge of the fountain. In addition to the wad of money, her carrier bag contained my old sponge bag, which has passed into her possession during my absence. Not even I can fail to see how thoroughly she has scrubbed the once squalid article. Now, under Lieschen's auspices, it is filled to overflowing, and I gaze in wonder at the uppermost layer of the small utensils she has arranged inside it in accordance with some system unfamiliar to me. She takes out a reel of thread and winds some around my finger so tightly that it clamps the edges of the wound together. I don't care to look at my bleeding flesh, so I stare instead at the open bag and try, in a sort of competition with myself, to discern and name as many as possible of the objects jammed together inside. Now that the zip is completely open, relieving them of lateral pressure, they have sagged apart. A dainty little red plastic comb is poking out and jutting over the edge. I try to push it back, but my clumsy left hand nudges the sponge bag off balance. It falls to the ground, and its multitudinous contents go tumbling across the paving stones.

My left cheek is stinging, my left ear buzzing, and even my left eye, of which Lieschen's vigorous slap caught only the lower edge, feels oddly invigorated. The upper lid has definitely lifted. It is once more lying taut across my eyeball – though only, I'm sure, while the shock persists – as though the impact of the blow has reminded it of its former position. Doc Zinally has subjected it to prolonged examination on each of my visits since the trouble began, using strange, old-fashioned instruments. My face has been painfully nipped with clamps and scanned through huge lenses mounted on mobile frames. Zinally has always responded evasively when asked why my lid is paralysed and whether it will get worse. He tends to hold forth in a digressive way that stifles further questions and defies contradiction – for instance, by making oracular pronouncements about the obscure antecedents of the Germanic race and lamenting the fact that it lingered too long in its first home east of the Black Sea. It always sounds as if he's trying to trace my eye complaint back to that dark, prehistoric period. Possibly to console me, Zinally likes to explain it away as an inherited racial defect, a belated consequence of regional inbreeding. I sense that Lieschen is looking at me. Still refreshed by her slap in the face, I try to return her gaze with comparable vigour. I don't succeed, but our visual exchange lasts long enough for me to gather that the girl expects me to get up and walk on.

We're waiting for Spaik, and I relish the sight of you waiting for him. You're standing at the window overlooking the street. Your right hand, the one that wears the ring taken from Spaik's mummy, is holding the curtains an inch or two apart. We know that the ninth anniversary of the Great Gahis's death will be celebrated come daybreak. We've been told several times during our twenty-four hours in the city, most recently by Freddy, that all foreigners will be spending this problematical day in a place of safety, so Spaik is bound to come home soon. You say you can sense he's already on his way. I pass you the plastic bottle we found in the refrigerator. Having drained it in three quick swigs, you shut your eyes and shudder. The little metal components of your necklace tinkle. The ugly bottle must have contained some of the legendary *zuleika* brandy little Calvin tried to tempt us with. We sight an old Gahist coming along the street. His lone figure is the first we've seen since standing at the window. He's limping, but he manages to lend his step a hint of determination in spite of the trouble his right leg is giving him. As the old man draws nearer, we can hear through the crack in the window how firmly he plants his hobnailed boots – even the one on the foot of his game leg. We know from Freddy that his hooded cloak is a form of pilgrim's attire. His face is concealed by a curious mask designed to protect the pilgrim from noxious emanations of all kinds, the miasma of evil thoughts included. He must be on his way to morning service, or making for the secret rendezvous from which the Gahists' demonstration will set off. In the light from the doorway of the adjoining house he pauses and leans against the doorpost, relieving the weight on his weaker leg.

I have to take another rest outside the door of our neighbour, Suqum the baker. I remove my hand from Lieschen's shoulder, lean against the doorpost, and try to take the weight off my aching leg. Lieschen had to support me for the last few steps. I bore down on the girl's neck and shoulders with the whole of my right arm, not just my hand. I fail to understand how she can have grown tall enough to support me without my noticing the change in her over the years. She waits patiently until I'm ready to go on. Tomorrow, she says, when the ninth anniversary of Gahis's death is over, she'll take me to Doc Zinally by taxi. Reflected by the road surface, the light of dawn is mingling with that of the lamp above our door. I noticed the little card lying there when I came to a halt, but it's only now, as the stabbing pain in my toes subsides and a numb sensation predominates, that I ask Lieschen to pick up the little piece of pasteboard, which I think I recognize.

The elderly Gahist takes three laborious steps into the street and stoops to pick something up, apparently a slip of paper. Then he hobbles back into the lamplight and spends a long time holding it up in front of his eyes as if studying an inscription of some kind. We watch him. You see no more than I do, but then you abruptly ask me why Kuhl said nothing, not a word, about the ninth anniversary of Gahis's death, and why he didn't think it worth warning us that our stay in the city would coincide with such a potentially momentous occasion. I'm doubly surprised, first by my own failure to ask this obvious question, and secondly by the grave dereliction of duty this withholding of information so clearly constitutes. Whatever Kuhl's motive may have been, it will cost him his in-house job on our return. The old Gahist, having examined the slip of paper at length, laboriously stows it under his cloak. He raises the garment waist-high, and we see that he's wearing it over a pair of ordinary slacks. Then he hobbles to the corner of Spaik's house and disappears from our field of view. We expect to see him reappear outside the house next door. Instead, we hear the front door close.

I'm home. I had to lean on Lieschen once more and was towed to our door instead of reaching it under my own steam. Once in the dark hallway I flop down on the second

step and gather my strength for the climb ahead. Sitting at
the foot of the steep wooden stairs has become a favourite
habit of mine over the years. Hypnotic fatigue overcame me
at this spot the very first time I got home from Freddy's
Steam Bath in the small hours. Sometimes I merely drape
myself over the banisters for a brief doze. Usually, however,
I do what I'm doing now: sitting on the second step and
lapsing into a stupor from which I'm sooner or later roused
by a sharp crack or a rustle – noises that probably come
from the two rooms on the ground floor. I haven't entered
them since my early days in the house, so some sizeable
vermin may have nested there in the interim. I don't recall
what the rooms contain. I may have used them for storing
superfluous items of my deceased predecessor's furniture,
but I can really remember only one of the things the Italian
left behind: his bicycle, a unique and sensational contraption by local standards. For one dreamy moment I feel sure
I did wheel the handsome bike in there. However, the door
to the ground-floor rooms looks as unfamiliar to me as if I'd
never opened it in my life. Lieschen, who has made the
house her own far more comprehensively than I, is bound
to know what has accumulated in there. I hear footsteps in
my quarters upstairs: the ancient floorboards are com-
plaining gently. It never ceases to surprise me how lightly
the girl can tread in her heavy boots when she wants to be
quiet. I stand up, but I feel dizzy, and after toiling up three
stairs I flop down again and briefly shut my eyes before
making a renewed effort.

The old man is moving around in the rooms downstairs.

We hear him pull up a chair; then the TV starts to boom. Cautiously, we head for the door, but the old floorboards make a soft, plaintive sound. If it carries to the ground floor at all, the noise from the television ought to drown it. We hear a man's voice preaching in a forceful, almost reproachful tone – a voice that is doubtless capable of uttering dark prophecies. I glance at you. You shrug your shoulders and smile as if to say there's no need to understand every one of this city's mental aberrations. Like me, you find it enough to surmise that it may be Spaik, his Western obesity squeezed into an exotic costume, who's sitting in front of one of his videos. Gahis's sermon seems to be nearing a climax. He breaks into a kind of rhythmical chanting, faster and faster, higher and higher. Ugly, effeminate, and hysterical, it culminates in an almost canine howl. There follow – part of the recording, it seems – a noise like the ripping of cloth and a dull thud. You reach for the doorhandle, and I nestle against your back in readiness to steal out on the landing with you. But an inexplicable sound causes us to draw apart abruptly. I glimpse the white encircling your irises, and, in an access of fear that isolates the pair of us as never before, you gaze into my own eyes, which must be just as widely dilated. As if from nowhere, a frightful din has invaded the room, a roar that quickly swells, then terminates in a clatter. You are the first to identify it. You shake off the paralysis that has gripped us both, go back inside the room, and draw aside the tapestry concealing the pneumatic post tube. When you open the flap a residue of pressure escapes with a vicious hiss. I unscrew the cylinder with shaking hands. Inside we find –

what else were we expecting? – the white-inscribed, absurdly misspelt piece of rubber announcing that transmissions have been discontinued for good. We look at each other with narrowed eyes. Whoever the sender of this communication may be, a tenant or old Spaik himself, we'll make him pay for the humiliating disparity between the meagreness of his message and the magnitude of our fear.

27 Love of Life

It's broad daylight, and Spaik knows that his right fore-finger is past saving: that scrap of flesh and bone will be lost to him for ever. He's enthroned in the television armchair with his hand, wrapped in a towel, resting on the back of the chair above head-height. Blood has soaked through the layers of towelling, dripped on to his scalp, and trickled through the hair on to his forehead, where it has congealed. No fresh blood is appearing. Despite the size of the wound, which has been torn open for a second time, the injured blood vessels have resealed themselves in a marvellously automatic way, with the aid of swollen tissue and coagu-lation. Doc Zinally has promised Spaik on the phone that he will bring all he needs to amputate the finger in a pro-fessional manner. Spaik is quite calm. Before subsiding into his TV chair, he used his uninjured left hand to scrape together such of Doc Zinally's colourful assortment of tablets as had accumulated beside and beneath his bed in recent years. He even managed, with puckered lips, to suck up the inaccessible pills and dragées that had rolled into the cracks between the floorboards.

It proved difficult to get in touch with the doctor by phone. Lynch Zinally found it a perceptible effort to concentrate on Spaik's account of what had happened; not even a description of the lacerated finger seemed to kindle his professional interest. Zinally had no desire to listen, merely to talk. Having sat glued to the television since early that morning, he was itching to unburden himself to some rational soul. Two news channels had started transmitting live reports from the city at dawn. The Gahists had launched their assault on Libidissi airport before daybreak. Warned of the impending attack during the night, the international security organizations and the local authorities had coordinated their efforts with unwonted speed and assembled all available personnel and mobile combat equipment at the airport. The suspicion that the Gahists had betrayed their own plans so as to guarantee a bloodbath of maximal proportions was now regarded as a certainty.

The first wave was spearheaded by experienced Old Gahists. Greybeards who had once, during the early days of resistance to the occupying power, performed legendary service as planters of bombs and dagger-wielding assassins, they stood like figureheads on the bumpers of their makeshift armoured cars. Most of the vehicles that trundled toward the first line of defence, the white tanks of the international defence force, were shopkeepers' delivery vans sparsely protected with planks and sandbags. The Gahist high command had set up a satellite link immediately before battle commenced, so the first television pictures were fed into the worldwide networks as soon as the opening shots were fired. The attackers had sneaked video cameramen into their foremost ranks, where they took first-class pictures heedless of the danger to life and limb. The cassettes were conveyed to camouflaged mobile transmission trucks by relays of runners. Shortly afterwards, a television camera mounted in a captured tank began to broadcast live.

Finally, when the dawn was at its loveliest, so Doc Zinally's telephone voice recounted between staccato sobs, the Gahists had sent their Young Guards into action: youths from the Goto, from the tenement buildings on the city's outskirts and the impoverished villages of the Northern Range. The helmets surmounting their slender bodies had looked like mushrooms, said Zinally. Armed with a motley assortment of international weaponry and specially trained to fight in small detachments, they achieved a breakthrough at terrible cost. The airport's defenders beat a panic-stricken retreat. Heavy equipment, including tanks, guns, and rocket launchers, fell into the Gahists' hands and were promptly turned against their former owners. US Marines and paramilitary units of the People's Militia succeeded in establishing a new defensive perimeter round the former military airfield and held it for a good hour. Towards midday, however, these positions were also overrun in spite of heavy air support. The head of the notorious Section 9 of the People's Militia, himself one of Gahis's comrades-in-arms some decades ago, held the military airfield's massive control tower against the Young Guards with his personal henchmen and a few dozen GIs who had become separated from their units. In the end, however, this veteran of the civil war and gallant member of the secret service fell prey to a bomb dropped too close for comfort by a US Marine pilot. The tower, Zinally reported, was still blazing.

Spaik listens for sounds from the roof space. Sometimes he thinks he can hear Lieschen's TV or one of her mumbled songs, but he isn't sure; loss of blood is making his ears ring. What he takes to be the rise and fall of a distant human voice may only be a product of lack of sleep or the onset of unconsciousness. Lieschen has probably been asleep for ages, quite unaware of what happened after she came home.

When the cylinder came thundering down the pneumatic tube, louder than ever before, it jolted Spaik out of his strange stupor on the ground floor. Startled, he recovered his wits in an instant and found himself standing once more at the foot of the stairs, some of which he thought he'd already climbed. The door to his living room opened in the darkness above. He heard footsteps, soft, overlapping footsteps indicative of the presence of more than one person. A recollection of his successor came flooding back from very far away, and sudden concern for Lieschen knotted something inside Spaik, some muscle behind his ribs, in a way that caused him unprecedented physical pain. He ducked into the shadows beneath the stairs, hitched up the *kuud* with his left hand and used his right, now doctored by Lieschen, to extract the lady's pistol. His fears for the girl's safety helped him to insert his heavily plastered finger into the trigger guard. He braced his head against the underside of the rough wooden treads, trying to attain some measure of composure, but it was no good, an awful sense of shame made him tremble: preoccupied with his peripheral aches and pains, he'd let Lieschen go upstairs on her own. The staircase's wooden substructure transmitted the flexing of the treads to his skull. Now that the two smilers were descending the stairs to the accompaniment of a faint tinkling sound which he knew without being able to identify it, he had no idea what his successors had done to Lieschen – or what they would do to her once they had immobilized him, crippled as he was in hand and foot, for evermore.

Noon sunlight penetrates the grimy window panes, causing Spaik's TV chair to cast a narrow shadow north-ward. His back detaches itself from the wickerwork. He aims his right ear at the ceiling, then his left. He has heard a scraping sound coming from Lieschen's domain – the bottom of her latrine bucket, probably. The idea fills him with embarrassment. Last night in the marketplace, his cheek still stinging from Lieschen's slap, he had watched her carefully, deliberately gather up the scattered contents of her sponge bag and replace them in accordance with her special system. His gaze roamed over the numerous small objects. Several tiny but meticulously sharpened pencil stubs caught his eye, as did a fat white India rubber, a nail file with a shiny mother-of-pearl handle, two pairs of nail scissors, two audiotapes without cases, a small book with a gilded fore-edge, sundry combs, a strange, oval elec-tric light bulb, a delicate cross-notch screwdriver, and a glass flask with a rubber bulb, which had fortunately sur-vived its landing on the paving stones. And then Spaik spotted the cartridge. Together with one or two other items, it had ended up near the base of the fountain and was lying almost exactly midway between the toes of his shoes. He saw at once that it was of the right calibre: small-arms ammunition dating from the middle of the World War century, and he needed only one such round to reload his twin-barrelled handgun. He made a mistake when he bent down to pick it up. His thumb and his forefinger, which Lieschen had plastered for a second time, closed on a little cylinder that crackled at their touch. It was probably attributable to the weakness of his left eye, to his defective stereoscopic vision, that he missed the cartridge at first and grasped instead an object of roughly similar shape and size: an aid to hygiene, a cylinder of cotton wool wrapped in cellophane.

The smilers had descended the stairs side by side. Shoulder to shoulder – striding along in step seemed to have become an ingrained, unthinking habit with them – they turned toward the door that led to the ground-floor rooms. The range was short, the downstairs passage sufficiently well lit by the little window in the door to the inner courtyard. Spaik took half a pace out from under the stairs, raised his right arm, and fired twice at their broad backs. A little while later, when he had dragged himself upstairs and, shaken by an endless fit of the giggles, bent over the washbasin to run some water over his hand and the gun, he saw what had happened to his own flesh: the first shot had burst the lower barrel completely, and a jagged piece of steel had ripped his forefinger open yet again, this time to the bone. It was a genuine miracle that this lacerated digit had succeeded in pulling the trigger past the second detent and loosing off the second round, the one from the upper barrel. Spaik managed to wrench the finger out of the trigger guard under the running tap, his nose and eyes running just as copiously. The first shot had hit the right-hand smiler fair and square. His body slammed into the door as if he'd taken a final leap at it, then slid to the floor and lay still. Spaik didn't miss the left-hand smiler either: hit in the arm, he staggered to the front door intent on escape. Spaik last saw him as the door yawned open, excellently illuminated by the overhead lamp whose glow was now mingling with the light of dawn. The young man tottered outside in a kind of self-embrace, clasping his left elbow with his right hand. Spaik even made out the ring on his hand, a ring set with a big, dark stone, before the door swung to and blotted out the fugitive's image.

Spaik gets up again. Laboriously, with his swaddled right hand on his head, he shuffles to the edge of the TV chair and uses his left hand to heave himself out of the dip in the cushion, intending to set off in search of some scissors. He wants to cut the *kuud* off his body before Zinally turns up. Spaik isn't sure if he possesses any scissors. The last ones he can recall – with futile clarity – were lying on the glass top of Kuhl's desk. Kuhl's hands had toyed with them for quite a while during their final conference at the Bureau, immediately before Spaik's departure. There was really nothing more to say. The car that would take him to the airport was waiting downstairs, but Kuhl, for no discernible reason, delayed shaking hands. Spaik had been watching his controller's fingers. Having replaced the scissors on the desk, Kuhl proceeded to play with a long pencil. He had ugly hands, speckled on the back and threaded with prominent veins. The knuckles looked swollen, as if heralding the first onset of gout. Eventually Kuhl stood up and promised to keep an eye on Spaik from afar. Somehow it struck a false note, as if the experienced controller had erred in his choice of words. To bridge the ensuing gulf of embarrassment, Spaik concentrated entirely on the handshake. Kuhl's right hand came across the desk towards him, but before he could clasp it without hesitation he noticed an unusual little feature – one that promptly aroused his utmost revulsion: a bluish, bulging vein in the angle between the thumb and forefinger of Kuhl's hand was throbbing like a pulse. It had a life of its own. And, when their hands clasped each other firmly, Spaik seemed to feel this pulsation transmitted, like a contagion, to his own extremity.

There are no scissors to be found. Spaik should have asked Lieschen, but he's loath to disturb her. She must be catching up on the sleep she was deprived of last night. When Spaik came upstairs with blood all over his hand, the murmur of Lieschen's television set greeted him as he pushed the door open. She turned it off when the jet from the tap sluiced the first of his blood into the washbasin. The smilers had let the girl pass unscathed. He'll have to manage without scissors and Lieschen's help. One of the kitchen knives is pointed and sharp enough to half rip, half cut the *kuud*'s woollen fabric. Leaning against the sink, Spaik sets to work. It's a difficult and arduous business because his left hand is unused to wielding a knife. He also finds that the muscles of his left eye are quite incapable of focusing the lens for a close-up view of himself. The lid refuses to close by itself, so he's compelled to lay the knife aside and press it shut with his fingers to enable him to operate one-eyed.

Spaik cuts the *kuud* off his body at last. Relieved, he hobbles back to the armchair. His rooms look deceptively big and bare. Halfway there, at the foot of Lieschen's ladder, he notices that one of the rungs has snapped and comes to a halt. The wood is lying in pieces on the floor-boards. Spaik picks up the largest fragment, which has a porous, worm-eaten consistency. He crumbles it into dust and fibres between his thumb and forefinger. He still remembers making the ladder, having bought all he needed at the local market: hammer, saw, nails, lengths of timber. The reddish wood, a slow-growing indigenous pine, was so hard that the saw soon became blunt and he bent one nail after another. Lieschen had sat in the television armchair, watching him at work and playing with her long, incredibly mobile toes. It was their first day together. Spaik didn't even know if she could speak, and his own Piddi-Piddi was so poor that he preferred to speak it only with foreigners. He had taken the child on a tour of the rooms and shown her the most important items: the lavatory, the tap in the kitchenette, the refrigerator. The hardness of the wood drove him to despair. He swore in German. Useless with his hands, he was running out of nails, and it looked as if he wouldn't finish the ladder that day. At length he dropped the hammer and looked up at the hatchway he was trying to reach. And that was when he noticed that Lieschen had started to hum. It was really more of a low growl, throaty and unmelodious, but it appealed to him, perhaps because it had nothing, absolutely nothing, to do with his failure and his imprecations.

Doc Zinally enters without knocking. Spaik has heard him clumping heavily up the stairs and the banisters plaintively creaking as he hauls himself up by them. Zinally comes over to the television armchair with the big black medical bag in his right hand and a small rectangle of yellow pasteboard in his left. Spaik recognizes it as one of Calvin's fortune-telling cards, doubtless the one he found in the street at dawn and must have mislaid on his way upstairs. He vainly tries to remember the nine-word aphorism. He read it in the light of the lamp next door, and the mysterious ambiguity of the words, whose cadences were skilfully imitative of Gahis's own rhythms, had made him think indulgently of Calvin's dubious art. Zinally deposits his bag on the floor. Then he draws himself up and, without a word, greets his patient with an upraised arm. Spaik is so touched by this simple gesture on the part of an American in exile that, in a feebly jocular fashion, he raises his own right arm as high as he can. The crimsoned towel flops into his lap, but he doesn't lower his hand. He not only returns the salutation accorded him by the doughty doctor, a devotee of Gahis and probably the last thoroughgoing racist in existence, but whispers that old-fashioned, monosyllabic German greeting which, if divested of its malign historical associations, would be more apt than any other to make us feel at one with life.